The Horde Without End

The World Without End, Book 2

Nazarea Andrews

Nazarea Andrews

Summary: With her brother missing, Nurrin teams with Finn O'Malley to find him in a world full of zombies and secrets.

978-0-9894799-6-7
1. Zombies. 2. New Adult. 3. Romance.

For information, address
14207 Ridge Court Upatoi GA 31829
www.nazareaandrews.com

Edited by Rachael Bateman
Cover design by The Illustrated Author
Cover art copyright©: Nazarea Andrews
Ebook Formatting by Ink in Motion

Nazarea Andrews

Books by Nazarea

After The End:
Edge of the Falls

The University of Branton:
This Love
Beautiful Broken
Sweet Ruin
Fractured Perfection (Fall 2014)

The World Without End:
The World Without A Future
The Horde Without End
Book 3 (2015)

Beyond Neverland:
Girl Lost
Forever Found: A Novella (Fall 2014)

Nazarea Andrews

Part 1. The Beauty of Breaking

We live without guarantees, in a time when loss is the norm. We are not given the luxury of falling apart.

-President Buchman, addressing Haven 1.

There is a world of strength waiting to be discovered in her moments of weakness.

-Finn O'Malley

Chapter 1. Broken Pieces

She hasn't cried. She doesn't cry for me—but I know how fragile she is.

I want to break her. I want to push her hard enough to see her shatter. I want to see the shards of her on the ground.

How fucking beautiful would she be, when she put herself back together? She would. Nurrin is too stubborn to do anything but survive.

Nurrin is a first, born to a world of death. She is innocent of the life before the change. She has never known anything but Hale Halls, razor wire, and walls. She has never known she could be anything but a survivor.

I watch the sun rising over the canyon. In another world, people might have exclaimed over the beauty, stared at it in wonder.

To me, the red-washed sky means only one thing: it's almost time to leave.

I glance over my shoulder. She retreated to the sleeping area a few hours ago, after we fought over leaving immediately. I think there is a part of her that hopes Collin will come back. A supply run wouldn't be completely unjustified.

My lips twist.

Collin wouldn't leave the Hole, not unless he had to. Not when he knew that it's the only place I would take Nurrin. He's gone because something is wrong.

Chapter 2. Making Plans

She's awake—I know she is, because as soon as I leave the cave entrance, she's poking her head out of the bedroom. Her eyes are suspiciously red, but she doesn't look as breakable as a few hours ago.

She does look tired.

"What are we doing?" she asks, her voice raspy.

"Do you think you're up to travel?" I ask, letting disbelief and disgust tint my tone.

Nurrin doesn't answer. She steps past me, her curling blonde hair brushing my arm as she snatches her gun and long knife from the table. I spent a few mindless hours cleaning everything last night. I catch her wrist as she pulls back, the one holding her knife, and Nurrin hisses slightly, a furious noise. "Don't play games, O'Malley," she says quietly. "I'm going to find my brother."

"I won't go out there if you aren't at a hundred percent. Do you understand that? I won't take you out there on some ill-advised suicide mission."

Anger flashes in her eyes, and she jerks free of my grasp. "What the hell do you think this is going to be? We have no clues to where he is—we're going out there with nothing to go on. Ill-advised is the least of what we're doing."

I laugh, and she wheels on me, her eyes wild. "You know something. What the fuck are you not telling me? Do you know where they are?"

"You trusted me, yesterday," I say quietly. Her eyes narrow, and she snorts. I want to laugh, but I swallow it and stare at her. "I'll find Collin. We were partners long enough that I have some ideas."

That's a lie, but her shoulders drop and her eyes brighten, a little. She's hesitant to trust me—but she wants to.

Hope. It's a wretched bitch.

"Collin wouldn't leave unless he had to. And he had the bike—we might be able to track him."

"Where would he go?" she asks.

Always the fucking questions. Even though they are warranted—justified—they irritate me. "Get your gear. I'm going to pack what food we have left."

Worry flashes in her eyes. "Why? Won't we come back?"

I look at her and blank my expression. It's not going to help to give her anything to pounce on. I can't face her questions right now—even if I had the inclination, we don't have the *time.*

"No questions, Nurrin," I say sharply. She gives me that annoyed look, but it's a step up from the hopeless fear that's been in her eyes since she realized Collin was gone.

She mutters a curse under her breath, and I smirk as she goes to do what I say. The amusement fades as I stare at the scratch on the table. It's cryptic. Three hurried gouges slashed in half by a fourth. An *i*, with a diagonal slash over it.

I had it covered with weapons, and she was too crazed with worry and fear to think to look—but I know the way Collin's mind works, and the protocol of Wall Walkers.

And Collin isn't so fucking stupid to leave without some kind of breadcrumbs.

The problem is that it's *just* a breadcrumb.

I push aside the niggling fear that Collin is running from a live infection, that taking Ren after him is putting her in danger.

It doesn't matter—she'd never tolerate being left behind. And if I did, it would just mean both of them would be missing, because she would bolt as soon as I was gone.

Doesn't mean I'll take her out without some kind of ground rules. I manage a grin. She'll be pissed.

"Nurrin," I yell, "get your ass out here."

"Fuck off, O'Malley," she grumbles without any real heat. She comes back out, and I take a quick look. She's changed into leather zom gear. It conforms to her ass, follows the curves of her pert breasts.

Shit.

The girl has to be carrying five different weapons, her brother and boyfriend are missing, and fucking her is *still* a bad idea.

So why can't I get her out of my system? I had hoped Lissel—I hiss and shove that thought aside. "Can you fit anything else in your bag?" She nods and brings it to the table. I shift so the marks are hidden and push some MREs to her. Her nose wrinkles, but she obediently loads them into her bag.

In minutes, we're done—it's almost disturbing how well we work together now.

"Weapons?" I ask shortly.

She huffs, but rattles them off. I nod and pass her a few hand grenades. "I'm driving, so I'll need to you cover us. Can you handle that?"

She gives me a flat stare. I arch my eyebrows, and she pockets the grenades.

There is something undeniably sexy about seeing Nurrin shove grenades into her leather pockets while a garrote is wrapped around one wrist and throwing stars hang from her waist. She catches my eye and gives me a grimace. "What?"

"You seem more together than I expected," I say. "I'm wondering how much is an act. Are you going to fall apart out there?"

Anger flickers in her eyes—that's fine. I don't care what she uses to keep from falling apart, to keep herself together and moving forward. As long as she does.

"I want my brother. I'll hold together for as long as it takes to find him," she says flatly.

"He could be dead, Nurrin," I say. Pain spasms across her face, and I should look away—no one should see something that intensely private. I don't. I watch her, fascinated.

"He could be. But he's not. Collin has survived twenty years—no zombie will kill him. Now get your shit and let's go."

"You know what the rules are—out there you obey without questions."

She snorts. "Fuck your rules, O'Malley. My brother is out there—you can help me find him, or you can get the hell out of my way. Those are *my* rules."

"That's a good way to get yourself dead," I shoot back.

Nurrin's expression goes blank. "Do you really think I care?"

She turns away before I can respond, but the question does its job—it tells me exactly how depressed she is, just how far she's fallen.

Nurrin isn't suicidal—she's too much of a survivor for that maudlin shit—but she is hopeless, and that could be worse.

"Let's go," I say.

Chapter 3. Topside

The cliff is swarmed with infects. All the ones near the Canyon when she started screaming last night are still here. A handful have fallen over the edge—I watched them tumble to the rocky bottom of the cliff during the night, but I can hear the screams and the quick darting steps as they circle the truck. Once, I hear the rattle of metal and a furious shriek—one apparently wandered too close to the razor wire.

Ren is pressed against my back, her entire body shaking with the need to fight. I draw my sword carefully and glance at her. She gives me a tight smile, and I nod once.

And we explode off the path.

The first zom screams as it sees us, and I feel the wind whistle past my face as Nurrin takes the cliff top, a throwing star embedding in the infect's throat, slicing deep. I jerk its head forward, onto the blade, and it goes limp as the razor edge slices into its spinal column.

Then the other infects are too close to think, and I'm twisting through them, leading with my sword. I can hear her shouting and cursing as she slams her blade into one infect after another. I hear it, and distantly I care—but really, the only thing that matters in this moment is killing and making sure we don't end up shoved off the damn cliff.

I whip around, my sword slicing through a rotten neck, and smile as gore sprays. "Truck," I shout. Ren growls behind me, a sound laced with annoyance more than anger.

She sounds nothing like the dead—too full of life. I glance at her, unable to resist. A zom screams, and I smirk, twisting away from Ren to slam my knife under its chin, burying it to the hilt in rotten brain matter. I shake the viscous matter from my hand and whistle sharply. Draw their attention from Ren. I bring my sword in front of me as they focus on me, away from Ren. She makes a face, annoyed, and I force my expression to go flat. She doesn't have to like it—I don't actually expect her to like it—I just need her to work with me and get the truck started.

Watching us, she makes her way to the waiting truck. I shout as she opens the door, and the nearest zom screams, lunging at me. I slide under the attack, slicing up. And stop thinking.

The only time I can turn off my brain is when I'm fighting the infects, because it doesn't take anything more than cut and slice and stay the fuck out of range of their teeth. That is easy—they don't demand anything, answers I refuse to give.

This is simple.

I give myself over to the ease of it all and fight my way through the infects. I'm vaguely aware that she turns on the truck, that I could fight my way to it—that I'm supposed to—but

I'm more focused on the fight. Until there is nothing left to kill, and I stand, panting, in a circle of the dead.

For a long minute, I just stare, slowly coming back to myself. Then the door to the truck cranks open. Ren pops out, standing on the step rail, a tiny thing dwarfed by the massive truck, bristling weapons. She gives me an arch look. "You feel better?"

Always with the fucking questions. I shake my blade, bend to wipe it off on the only clean scrap of cloth I can find on the dead. Sheath it and stalk over to where she's leaning out of the truck. Give her a flat smile.

"Let me guess," she says dryly, "you're driving."

At least the girl can learn.

Chapter 4. Roadside Revelations

We're driving for maybe five minutes—long enough that the canyon has vanished behind us and Nurrin has begun to get twitchy—when she finally asks. I'm surprised it took her this long.

"Where are we going? They could be anywhere."

I deliberately keep my gaze ahead. "I know where he was heading."

On her side of the truck, Nurrin is a trembling ball of outrage. I don't need to look at her to know she's glaring, or that hope has sparked in her eyes, however briefly.

"What are you talking about?"

"Collin carved a message in the table. He's headed to Haven 9."

"Why there?" she demands, her voice going shrill.

"Because it's close. I'd guess that Dustin's infection spread and he had no choice—there's no sign that there was a breach, but he'd get out of here, if it meant saving Dustin's life or buying him a little more time while they wait for our return."

"Why wouldn't he just say that? Why make it so fucking difficult?"

I slide a glance at her. She's staring out the window, fury etched on her face.

She won't like this.

"Because his sister is a First. And because I'm his partner—*we* both have enemies, and he can be used as leverage against either of us."

"He was alone there, Finn," she says. I hear her hesitation, though, and flash her a quick smile—she isn't asking about why I would have enemies. Not now, anyway.

"Doesn't matter—Collin is smart. He found a way to tell me what I needed to know."

"Then why did you say that, about him being dead? If you know where he was going?"

I stare out the windshield, at the dust that is sweeping the canyon edge. It's hot and dry and carries the hint of smoke and decay.

Everything smells of decay, these days.

"Because it's a long way from here to Haven 9. And there are a lot of obstacles between us and him. Because the Wide Open is full of the dead, and we both know they're changing—and Collin was traveling with a live infection—even if he could get to 9, they could have thrown him and Dustin into Q."

She flinches, and I try to get a grip on my temper. Being angry with her won't do anything, and I can't afford to fight with her—right now, nothing matters but finding Collin.

"You didn't tell me what you were planning, when we left 18."

My grip tightens a little on the steering wheel, and she sighs. "Are you going to keep me in the dark this time, too? Because if you feel the burning need to fuck and murder an Alderman, I'd like a little warning this time."

I snort, banking my anger. She's furious, and cool indifference is the only way to handle Nurrin's anger.

"She wasn't supposed to die," I say. Not that this time will actually make it through her thick skull. I'm tired of repeating the same shit to her.

"What was she supposed to do? Jump to safey? You were dragging her into a horde, with no recourse to get home."

I bristle. "Haven 18 will fall. If it hasn't already, it will within the month. I was getting her out of a sinking ship. Is that so fucking wrong?"

"You killed her."

I nod. "But I gave her a clean death—she was dead as soon as she drew a knife on me."

She shudders. "She was dead as soon as you decided to fuck her."

Ah. That is the crux of it. The real issue she has with me killing Lissel.

"Sex doesn't mean anything, Nurrin. It's a biological need, and she met it. Doesn't mean I give a fuck about her or it."

"She loved you," she protests, shrilly.

I laugh at that. Because it's the classic mistake, and I'm not surprised that she's making it. Disappointed, but not surprised. "She didn't love me, Nurrin. She didn't fucking know me."

She looks at me, and I can feel the sympathy and pity coming off her in waves. It infuriates me, but I keep my grip on the steering wheel light as I twist to avoid a stack of freshly killed infects.

I wonder who bothered to stack them.

"No one knows you, O'Malley. You won't let anyone get to know you. Why is that?"

"Why do you still think I'll answer your questions?" I shoot back, and she flushes, leaning back in her seat. "I don't give a fuck if people know me, Nurrin. Frankly, it makes staying alive easier when I don't have to worry about idiots who think they *know* me trying to save me." My tone is mocking, calculated to get a reaction.

She laughs, and I flick a quick look at her. "You told the Alderman Melinda that they should live—that hiding from the disease was only choosing a slow death. But you hide from the whole world. What are you choosing, by doing that?"

She doesn't wait for a response. Instead, she props her feet on the dash—something she knows I despise—and leans back, closing her eyes.

Chapter 5. Holed Up

When the dead came back and the world went to hell, there was a lot left behind. Big cities didn't fare well—Houston burned for two months during the first wave of infection, and Atlanta didn't just burn, it smoldered, the ash of radiation and infection a true testament to the magnitude of the change.

But small town America didn't fare so badly. Whole towns were untouched by the first wave of infection, escaped it altogether—until the refugees and the government swarmed in and shoved everyone behind Haven walls.

Sometimes, when I'm drunk and feeling nostalgic, I wonder what would have happened if they hadn't. If they had let nature and humanity live out together—if we could have stopped the disease if we all fought it, instead of just the ragtag army they sent to fight the Battle of the East.

Not that it matters. The government made their evac orders, and the American people, convinced the world was ending and their government had their best interests at heart, obeyed.

The rest has been a slow march toward extinction.

I slow as we ease into the ghost town, and Nurrin blinks, stretching in her seat as she comes awake.

"Where are we?"

"No idea. Some town between the canyon and 9. We need to stop for the night."

She leans forward, scanning the streets. "I don't see anything out there."

"No, I haven't seen an infect in a few hours," I say quietly. It's still a while before sunset, but the city is the perfect place to hole up for the night, and I don't want to chance being stuck on the road without a bolt-hole.

And there is the slim possibility that we can scavenge a little.

"That one," she says, and I glance at the house she's pointing to. She's right, as much as it pains me to admit. It's on a wide swath of overgrown grass. A swing has collapsed into the rotten porch. It's decrepit and untouched—which makes it perfect. And a small forest of apple trees wave from behind it—fresh fruit wouldn't be the worst thing to stock up on.

Without saying anything, I turn the truck into the drive. Gravel pops under our tires, a few sticks snapping in the silence. I park a safe distance away—close enough to get to and from the truck safely, and far enough that we can make a quick escape if something is inside—and we sit there, eyeing it.

"How many rodents do you think are crawling around in there?" she asks finally.

"More than you'll appreciate."

She snorts. "I appreciate rat stew as much as any Haven girl, O'Malley."

My lips twitch, and I reach behind us to grab my crossbow. She checks the magazine on her 9mm and then slams it back in, chambering a round.

"Ready?" I ask softly. She flashes me a quick grin, and I shove the door open. Nurrin prowls out of her side of the truck, her gaze darting around nervously.

She's adjusted, too well, to being in the Wide Open.

It's a little unsettling how easily we gain the house. There is no sign of life—or the undead—as we move across the overgrown lawn and she reaches down, easing the door open carefully.

I step in quickly, scanning the room with my bow up. Nurrin steps in behind me, sniffing the air experimentally.

It's dry—musty and old, but there is no hint of rancid *badness* that clings to the infects.

"Did we actually find a Clean city?" she asks, her voice a little awed.

I shoot her a look. "Those are myths, Nurrin. Get your head on straight."

She flips me the bird, and I relax a little—she's not a hundred percent, and I can see the sadness in her eyes when I'm not needling her. But if I can still get a rise out of her, she's not too far gone, and that is something to hold onto.

We clear the house, finding nothing living or dead. Just an empty house, still carrying the weight of the people who abandoned it.

"I'm going to scavenge, while we still have some daylight."

She nods. "I'll get a safe room together."

It's what I would have told her to do—that she immediately moves to do so is a little disconcerting. I watch her for a moment, searching for something, and she rolls her eyes. Without a word, I stalk from the house.

The city is Clean. And I haven't seen one of those since we swept out of the East, retreating to the land the living had claimed.

There are always rumors of them. Even now, twenty years after the world fell apart, people still talk about Clean places—mountain tops and islands are popular—pockets of infection-less land. I used to think there were Clean islands. For half of that first year, I clung to the idea. But the fact is, they don't exist. ERI-Milan ripped through the entire world and nowhere—not even the poorest villages in the most remote countries—was able to escape the ravages of it. Not after it mutated outside of Atlanta.

But for the moment, the infects have abandoned the little town, and I prowl it unencumbered.

There isn't much to find—twenty years of decay and scavengers have left it at it's bare essentials, but I do find a few packs of water pures in an abandoned car and an old can of zom repellant. I grab both and hit a nearby RV.

It's the newest looking vehicle—a Ford ZTNK2300. The tires are flat-proof. Blood is caked to the side of the RV, and I wonder how long ago they—whoever they were—were killed. I bring the bow up again, my finger twitching on the trigger as I reach for the door.

The bang of it slamming against the outside is ridiculously loud, but nothing comes out screaming, so I duck into the vehicle.

It's fully stocked. Food and cases of water, a stack of batteries and powdered zom repellant, ammo and several guns. Even the mattress and pillow look sound.

Like whoever had been here stepped out for a breath of air, and never come back.

I think of the blood stain and shake my head—they probably did.

I should feel worse about pillaging from the dead—but in our world, it's necessary. You do what it takes to survive, and fuck the sensibilities of the dead, or stupid shit like decorum. Decorum won't kill a zom—but the rounds of ammo sitting in this RV will. I glance at the front of the ZTNK and see the keys there.

Fuck. I'm going to have to let her drive my fucking truck.

I see Nurrin, her blonde hair a pale shadow in the window, as I pull up. I can imagine what she's thinking—who the hell goes out to scavenge and comes back with an RV?

Part of me says to let it go—I don't need the damn thing.

Except that I don't know that. My influence is fading—it has been since I left Haven 1. There are people who hate me, more than I care to think about. And I have no idea what it will take to get Collin out of whatever mess he's found himself in.

I grit my teeth. She won't be happy about it—it'll slow us down and make us more conspicuous on the road, neither of which is ideal.

I grab my crossbow and climb out of the ZTNK, locking it behind me. We might be in an impossibly Clean town, but the Wide Open always holds a few surprises—and I didn't want this one wandering away in the middle of the night.

Nurrin is standing with her arms crossed over her chest when I walk up the creaking stairs. I glance past her into the room she's cleared. It's been cleaned, and she's set up for the night, laying out two sleep sacks, a couple of MREs, and bottled water. The room reeks of zom repellant, and the floors almost gleam. There is a small pile of curious rubbish, and I flick a glance at it. "I cleared the house," she says. "Where the hell did you find a ZTNK?"

"On the main street. I didn't see anything, and it'd been abandoned."

"And what happens when the people who were trawling in it come back and realize it's gone?"

"They'll manage." I shrug. I reach down and grab an MRE. Beef Strogenoff. Disgusting shit.

"Finn, I really don't think it's a good idea," she says softly.

I stare at her, a long stare. "Do you really think they'll be coming back?"

She flinches. "Yes. I have to believe they'll be back."

We're not talking about random strangers in the ZTNK anymore. But then, I don't think we ever were.

"I picked apples," she says, an abrupt change of topic. I glance at them—they're small and look hard, but it's fresh—looking ahead at a few days of MREs, anything fresh is nice.

"We should have stayed at the damn Casino," I mutter.

"Their food is definitely a step above ours," she agrees. I glance at her as she turns to set the apples down. Her ass has dust on it, smeared from her hands, probably, and there's a smudge on her arm—sometime between getting here and me coming back from scavenging, she's come out of her zom gear.

"What's in the RV?"

"It's fully stocked—looks like they were making a long trip. Ammo, food, clothes, survival gear—everything you'd need for an extended stint outside."

"Any clue where they came from?"

"Didn't look. But it'll be good for trading if we run into any trouble."

She glances back at me. "Won't your name be enough to get us through?"

Irritation sparks through me, and I take a deep breath, catching my temper before it breaks completely.

I grab the MRE she tosses to me and give her a blank look. "You're fishing again, Nurrin."

"No," she says. Her voice wobbles briefly. "I'm not fishing—I'm not playing games. I'm through with games, Finn. I need to find my brother."

"What do you think we're doing?" I ask sharply.

"You said once that the only thing that mattered was that you'd keep me safe and Collin safe."

I nod—I remember telling her that.

"You were right. That's all that matters. I don't give a fuck who you were, or what you did—I just care about getting to Collin before it's too late."

"We both want the same thing, Nurrin. I want him back, too."

She stares at me for a long tense moment, and then, “Why did you let him in? Of all the people in 8, why did Collin crack you?”

I remember that first day, walking into the training room. I hadn’t needed it—but the Commander had insisted if I were to Walk, I’d train with his men. So there I was, and Collin was leaning against a wall, watching with this little smile on his face. I didn’t know much about him, except two very important things: he survived the Turn, and he was Nurrin Sanders’ brother.

Even then, I knew who she was—a hot-blooded, spitting hellcat at fifteen. I’d been watching her from a distance since I arrived in 18, and I’d learned a lot.

Quiet. Unassuming. And fucking savage when she was threatened. One recurring theme was her brother. He had no life outside his sister and went through hell to keep her identity as a First under wraps.

I walked up and gave him a smirk. "How long do you think you can keep a First under wraps?"

His face had gone comically shocked, and then he punched me.

"O'Malley," she snaps, exasperated. I blink, staring. How long had I been lost in thought? "You know, it gets really boring when you refuse to talk about anything," she says grumpily. I shrug, and she snorts and settles across from me with her MRE.

Chapter 6. The Lies of a Clean City

She takes first watch. Even in a city with no evidence of infects, we're going to have a watch. Anything else would be stupid and irresponsible. When she wakes me for my watch, I stretch and murmur, "Anything?"

"No."

We don't say anything else as she crawls into her sleep sack, and I prop against the wall by the window, rolling my neck to work out the kinks. Slowly, silence eases back down on the little room.

I stare out into the darkness, trying to ignore the sound of her quiet, almost silent crying. The wind has picked up, and it shakes the trees outside, giving everything an eerie quality and making the shadows dance. But for all of that, it's quiet.

"We can leave," she says.

"Not in the dark, Nurrin. Suicide missions aren't my thing."

She makes an unladylike noise and rolls over.

A shrill scream splits the night, and she jerks upright. Even in the darkness, from the far side of the room, I can see the terror on her face, the wild, wide eyes. I put a finger to my mouth, and she nods. Shifts out of her sleep sack and crawls silently to my side.

The first zom appears from the trees, darting out of the depths of the apple orchard. She shivers, watching it, and doesn't see the second.

I do.

"Fuck," I whisper. She looks away from that first—it's almost to the house—and sees what I do.

Infects are pack animals. They travel in small groups—small being the key. There's a lot of speculation as to why—my theory is that they can't feed enough to sustain large groups. They happen, occasionally, especially when cities were falling in the East. But tey always splinter, a horde becoming smaller and spread out, manageable.

This though—

It's a horde.

And not just a horde—but the largest I've ever seen. It makes the mass of infects in Vegas, drawn there by the Order, seem small. It's bigger than the horde that enclosed the truck on our way back. They pour out of the trees by the hundreds, swarming the orchard and around the house. They aren't silent—not like the last horde we saw. This one is full of fury and hunger, their screams scraping along the walls of the house, filling up the little room until I'm sure it will drown out everything, the last sounds we ever hear. Nurrin mutters a low curse and clamps her hands over her ears, her eyes scrunched shut.

It's not an escape. There isn't one.

The worst part isn't the screams, or the sheer number of them. It's how new they are.

The horde moves with speed and fury, at an awkward, limping gate. Like the infection is still ripping through them, changing them.

I see Wall Walkers, snarling alongside the others.

She makes a low noise, almost a moan, and I shift, putting a hand to her lips.

They can't hear us—not over their own noise—and they probably won't be able to sniff us out over the reek of zom repellant. But it's still better to stay quiet until the horde has passed.

She slumps against me, and we sit like that for a long time, watching as they race by. Snap at each other. Scream in anger and hunger.

They're changing. ERI has always been highly adaptable—it was the miracle of the drug, and the reason it doomed us all. But their behavior is becoming a pattern.

Hordes, moving like they've scented the living, when there's no reason for it. Infects don't move like that unless they've narrowed in on a human. Even animal meat doesn't raise this kind of response.

I've known this was coming—that it was inevitable. I'm still not ready for it.

But at least the falling Havens make a little more sense.

Even after they have passed, we sit in silence, watching a few straggling infects scrambling after the main horde.

The silence, after the screaming fades, is startling. It wraps around us like a heavy blanket, broken only by her raspy breathing as she tries not to fall apart. I sink down and prop my crossbow against my knee. Glance across the window to meet her terrified eyes.

"What are they doing?" she asks, her voice shaking. My muscles clench, and I struggle to stay still. It's the last thing I want. But I can't have what I want.

"They're adapting," I say, looking away. "ERI-Milan is a highly adaptable virus. It looks like it's changed again."

"But why?" Nurrin sounds lost and broken—I hate that weakness in her voice, hate that I think less of her for it.

"Why do any of us adapt? They're trying to survive."

She opens her mouth to say something, and I roll my head to the side, staring out the window. "Get some sleep, Nurrin. What the infects are doing doesn't matter—tomorrow we have to get to 9."

I hear her inhale, probably preparing to argue with me. I flick a glance at her, and she bites down on whatever she's going to say. Snuggles deeper into her sleep sack, which she half drug over when the horde came through. I stare out at the darkness as she closes her eyes and drifts off to sleep, refusing to look at her.

The infects were fresh. That's the most troubling part of it—not the size of the horde. I've known for a long time that they outnumber us. But this is unprecedented. Even during the first wave of infection.

That first three months, while the world fell to pieces and the dead moved like a fucking plague, three of seven people were killed or changed. Those were your odds. Seven people walk into the apocalypse. Four make it out—if they're lucky.

Three billion died in three months. Then we got our shit together enough that we could fight back, pulling every defense we had into the fight and throwing up walls as quickly as we could. Havens went up faster than anyone believed possible—the first four were functioning within six months of the bombing of Atlanta.

Having the dead killing the living lit a fire under people's asses. Evac orders were sent, and we hid. The slaughter slowed after that.

By the time First Day rolled around for the first time, another billion were dead. The dead outweighed us by numbers—but we were fighting back and holding our own.

Fucking stubborn.

I shake my head, trying to dislodge the thoughts of another time, another life—back when I thought we could win this fight. Back when winning might have meant something. We all dreamed of something—going back to the world we had before Emilie died and everything changed.

The truth is there is no winning—no going back. The zombies are here—ERI-Milan is too prevalent and adaptable to kill completely. We will never reclaim the East. We will never be rid of the zombies.

We're all searching for something—a Clean place—but what we're really doing is waiting for the other shoe to fall.

And from the size of that fucking horde, I'm beginning to wonder if it already has and we're just not aware of it yet.

Chapter 7. Roadside Hazards

The truck ahead of me bobbles, riding the edge of the curb, and I tap my horn, annoyed. If she blows out one of my tires because she's fucking with the AC, I'm going to be pissed. She responds by flashing her brakes at me.

Smartass.

I don't like her in a separate car. There's no one to take point, for either of us. If we hit trouble—when, because it's always just a matter of time—there's no one to cover us. I'm used to being able to concentrate on the road, because she's riding shotgun, that little pistol of hers always in her lap.

A girl with a gun should not be such a fucking turn on.

But I've been a walking hard-on since she rolled out of her sleep sack this morning, her shirt tangled up and giving me a delectable view of her nipples, shadowed points under the thin cotton.

I remember what she felt like, under my hand in the club at the casino. I remember how she came alive, how she had crawled into my lap, a hot little bundle of want.

She might hate me. It might be the worst idea in a long line of bad fucking ideas. But there is no denying there's a hell of a connection between us.

I've always known there would be. It's the only thing that's kept me away from her bed all these years.

Nurrin isn't a Haven girl—not the kind I can fuck and forget. Even if I tried, I don't think she'd let me—she's the kind of girl that sinks into your pores, who comes screaming and wraps around your soul.

Which is a stupid fucking thought if I've ever had one.

The truck bobbles again, and I curse, shoving the ZTNK into high gear and pushing the throttle until I'm alongside her.

She's smiling, one leg propped on the seat as she nibbles on an apple and steers one handed. The window is down, whipping her hair around like a blonde tornado.

She looks free and unconcerned—the most carefree I've seen her since we left Haven 8. I let the window roll down and toss a bullet at her. She smirks at me, her eyes lazy and taunting. "Keep the damn truck on the road!" I shout.

She laughs, lazily flips me the bird, and hits the gas. I swallow my laughter as she pulls ahead of me, swerving into my lane to cut me off. I relax against the plush seat, staring at the taillights of the truck and trying to think about something other than why I want to fuck her senseless. And how—because I have a damn good imagination and—

A plume of dirt kicks up suddenly to the east. Too suddenly. I smack the horn. Three quick beats. She hits the brakes so fast I swerve, the ZTNK swaying alarmingly as I dodge the suddenly still Ford.

She's out and moving before I've stopped the ZTNK, exploding into the back of the RV with worry clear in her green eyes.

"Kill the truck," I order quickly. "Then take the roof of the ZTNK."

She nods, and I jerk on the trap door to the roof, letting the collapsible stairs fall down. There are three mounted gun turrets up here, and a weapons locker. I flip it open and grin at the sight of the grenades. The dust is getting thicker, moving closer, and across the empty plain, I can hear the sound of engines, the buzz like an annoying insect.

Nurrin is leaning into the engine of the truck, her ass in the air, and I whistle sharply. She shouts a curse then pops up, holding a greasy handful of spark plugs.

My truck isn't going anywhere.

"Nurrin, move your ass," I shout, and she turns back, lurching to the truck and almost climbing inside. I glance again at the cloud, and I can pick them out, a group of motorcycles darting across the plain, a few open backed Jeeps.

Fuck.

"Nurrin," I snarl again, and she's in, the RV door locking behind her. It's a steel reinforced door, made to be resistant for up to twelve hours of siege. There's no way they're coming in that way. I hear the clatter of her feet, and then she's at my side, stepping past me to grab a few grenades and tucking them into her pocket.

"Will they leave us alone?" she asks, checking her knives. I feed a string of bullets into the machine gun and click the safety off. Shrug.

The buzz has become a roar, and I step away from my gun and into Nurrin's space. She goes stiff as I put an arm around her, tugging her against me, my lips at her ear. “Sit down on the roof. Try to look non-threatening. Follow my lead, do you understand?"

“You are so fucking bossy," she grumbles, her breath against my neck punctuating the words. My grip tightens on her, and I shake her a little. She knocks my hands away, glaring. “I understand. I'll be your little windup toy, but I'll be honest, O'Malley. This shit is getting hella old."

I dismiss her complaint, turning the gun lazily to the south, and watch the motorcycles rumbling closer. Dust billows up around the RV and us as they prowl around the truck and race circles around the ZTNK.

Marauders. I watch them, looking for some clue to what kind they are—the type to be tossed out of a Haven for a criminal offense or the kind who just hates government control.

Some people are stubborn enough that they'll face the infects before they face the government controlling their life and world, even with the limited government we have now. It's not exactly sane, but it's their choice. And there is something vaguely tempting about it—the lure of freedom.

These though—they're not people looking for a bit of freedom. These are people who live on the edge of society because they can't abide by society's laws.

Before, people who broke laws were put in prison to keep them away from society and to carry out their punishment. But when we turned prisons into havens, we had to rethink the justice system.

It was pretty simple. Follow the rules, or be put in the Wide Open to take your chances with zombies.

It didn't get rid of crime entirely—nothing could do that—but it helped.

But the people who lived in the Wide Open, in traveling gangs, they were vicious, with no moral qualms and a survival streak a mile wide.

I let a smile stretch my lips. Because we have something in common.

The leader is a scrawny man with thin hair, sharp eyes, and enough weapons that I'm left wondering if he has a bit of an inferiority complex.

He grins up at us, a dangerous gleam in his eyes as he watches Nurrin's swinging legs. She looks bored and utterly unconcerned.

That's my girl.

I blank my face, and he laughs. "Nice tanks y'all got. Where you headed?"

"Haven 23," I say idly. "You?"

A laugh rumbles through the group. "We tend to drift, friend."

"Dangerous habit for these days," I observe.

"Necessity. Not everyone fits neatly into your havens. What happened to your truck?"

"Engine trouble. We'll get it fixed—no need to stop for us."

"Well. About that. You look like good people—well connected, and headed for a nice life in 23. Unfortunately, I can't say the same about my people. So we're going to even the odds a little." He grins. Like that kind of logic works. It didn't work before the zombies, and it sure as fuck doesn't work now.

Nurrin tenses, and I step close to her, pressing my legs into her back. She relaxes a little, and I look back at the scrawny leader.

"We can't help you," I say simply.

"That wasn't a request, pretty boy. Give us your ammo and food. We'll take the ZTNK. You get to keep your life and the truck."

Nurrin laughs, and the man's eyes dart to her, furious suddenly. I'm tempted to smack her for drawing their attention.

"I don't like their offer," she says, leaning back on her hands. She grins up at me, and I smirk. Cocky little girl.

"The other offer is you put up a fight—and we take it all, including you, blondie. After we kill your boy."

I throw the star without even thinking, without considering that it's a bad idea. It's instinctual, a quick flick of my wrist, and the flash of metal, the heavy thunk as it embeds in the tire of Rat-man's bike. Nurrin whistles, and I catch her by the arm, tugging her back. She scrambles to her feet, a solid presence behind me as I stare at the leader.

He's furious, and I consider that it was probably a bad idea to bait him like that. *Too late*.

"Last chance. Leave us alone," I say evenly.

"You have two guns and a few knives," Rat man snaps. "I have a gang of twenty experienced fighters. Do you really think you'll win this?"

I smile, a lazy twitch of my lips. "Only one way to find out."

Rat man sighs. "Take the damn RV. Don't damage it—and leave the girl untouched. I want her."

Fury flares in me. I shift Nurrin behind me, hear her soft huff of displeasure. "The girl is mine," I snap, and she makes a choked noise. Rat-man pauses. Stares at me. Around him, his people are uncoiling chains and grappling hooks. "You try to scale this wall, I'll throw you down. I promise I can outlast you."

"Not if I shoot you first," he says, pulling a gun. I laugh. I'm goading him—and I know I am. I bare my teeth in a parody of a smile.

"Fight me—even and fair. Winner takes the ZTNK. The girl goes free regardless."

Rat-man's expression twists to disbelief. "Why?"

I glance at Ren. She smirks and holds up a grenade. "Because I'll blow this fucking RV before I let you touch me."

His eyes narrow, and then he laughs. "Why not?"

I glance at her. "If anything happens, get the fuck out of here. Do you understand?"

She shakes her head slightly, and I growl, choking the noise off a second too late. "I need to know you'll get safe, Nurrin. Don't let that animal touch you."

Worry wars with anger, and she steps into me, hissing, "If you get yourself killed and leave me alone in the wide open, I will find your zombie ass and chain you in my basement until you rot. Do *you* understand?"

I let it all out, let everything I'm feeling into my eyes, for just a moment, and her eyes widen. She takes a breath, and I jerk her close, kissing her.

Because if I die, I'll do it with the taste of her on my lips.

For a split second, she's startled, unmoving. And then her hand comes up, fisting in my hair, her lips parting on a groan. I dip into her mouth, controlling the kiss, angling her the way I want.

She yanks on my hair, hard, biting my lip with just enough force that I hiss, and draw back.

Nurrin grins. "Go slay the dragons, O'Malley," she drawls. She turns away, all cool nonchalance, but I see the press of her nipples and the flush crawling up the skin of her neck.

Chapter 8. Fight It Out

People like talking. They like sitting down and hashing out whatever fucked up problem they've invented, talking about it until the issue is so muddled they can't remember what the fuck they sat down about in the first place.

I don't talk. And from the feral gleam in Rat-man's eyes, I know he doesn't either. I swing down the stairs and key open the steel door, triggering it to swing shut and lock behind me. I'll be out here alone—she won't rescue me if shit goes bad.

If she does, I'll kick her pretty little ass.

I grin, and then I step out, out onto the sand.

The gang is arrayed around us in a loose circle, and I give them a lazy grin. "You people gonna let him fight?"

One spits on the ground. "Why should we? Kill you now would be easiest."

A shot rings out, the ground exploding inches in front of the man's foot. He curses, stumbling back a few steps.

"Because if you interfere, she'll put a bullet in your head. She doesn't miss."

It's the only warning I'm going to give. I launch myself at Rat-man, who gives a low shout, jerking backward.

He's off balance and retreating. Already. This might be easier than I thought. I dart in, and he comes up swinging a knife. His gang cheers, a noise that recedes as the blade scores across my arm, a shallow cut.

It doesn't do anything but piss me off.

I glance down at the cut then lunge, tackling him. He punches at me, and I bat the blow aside, grabbing his knife hand a split second before he drives toward my ribs. I twist, hard, and Rat-man's eyes widen in pain. The knife clatters free on the road. I should let go now—but I don't. I keep twisting, until I feel the bones bending, and then a little farther.

His scream breaks the silence, and I smile, a cold smile. Grab a handful of his dirty hair and slam his head into the asphalt. Again. Again.

"Enough," a sharp voice shouts, and I blink. Blood is pooling under his head. I glance up at Nurrin—she's standing, a worried look on her face, her gun propped on one hip.

I give her a slow smirk and stand.

"You bastard," one of the men hisses, lunging at me. I pull my gun, shooting him point blank. Nurrin curses above me, and I step into their leader.

"Get the fuck out of here," I say softly. "Or I'll kill him. Do you understand?"

"What the hell is wrong with you?" one shouts, staring at their dead comrade. "You fucking killed him!"

I smile, a savage expression. "You stop me, threaten my life, my woman, and you have the fucking balls to stand here like I did something wrong? You're lucky I'm letting any of you leave."

"O'Malley," she yells, her voice urgent. I hear the scream a second later, faint but unmistakable.

Enough of this bullshit. "Take your trash and get away from us," I snarl. I turn and snap my fingers. Nurrin tosses the bag of spark plugs, and I snatch them from the air. She meets my eyes, briefly, and I see the worry, the concern before she shuts it down. The screams come again, and I turn to the truck.

Footsteps are my only warning, then the report of the gun. I glance back, and see another gang member on the ground, writhing.

"That wasn't a kill shot, little girl."

"No need to be excessive," she calls back. I laugh.

For some reason, that does the trick—the remaining gang members scramble for their bikes. I shove the spark plugs into place and slide into the truck.

Rat-man has been deserted. He's squirming on the ground, his eyes wide as he searches for his gang. I feel a flash of pity, but it's outweighed by the knowledge that he'll buy us time.

Another gunshot rings out, and I look over. Nurrin is leaning out the passenger side window, her gun pointed. Rat - man slumps, a neat bullet hole in the center of his forehead.

Idiot girl.

"Let's go, Nurrin!"

She rolls her eyes, slides into the driver's seat of the ZTNK. And we leave them all behind.

Part 2. The Lie of Hope

In reality, hope is the worst of all evils, because it prolongs man's torment.

-Friedrick Nietzche

"Hope is the reason we're alive. Because humanity was too fucking stupid to let it go."

Finn O'Malley

Chapter 9. Aimless Direction

The RV rattles around me, and it's not enough to kill out the fears dancing in my head.

Captured. Dead. Turned.

The litany repeats on a loop. I can't close my eyes without seeing Collin, broken and bleeding, one of the corpses in the bloody streets in front of the Stronghold. I've pictured him dead a thousand ways, dead and worse—infected.

In the Clean house, Finn thought I'd slept. I'd stared into the darkness until my eyes ached, until I thought I'd scream from the sitting still—there were so many things we could be doing, and waiting for daylight seemed like the most wasteful.

Every minute we spent not finding Collin was like a small slice of glass on my skin. Every breath aches, carrying the weight of guilt and the knowledge that we might never find him.

I'm following Finn because I have no direction of my own. Because sitting still would do nothing, and I would go slowly insane if I didn't do something, but on my own I would just curl into myself and pray the demons away. I'm following Finn on the fool's hope that he knows what he's doing, that my brother is alive and waiting for us in 9.

I don't believe it. Not really. But it's all I have to hold on to at the moment, so I clutch it like a lifeline, the only thing that is pulling me along on this aimless search.

Chapter 10. Preparatory Males

I can see the Walls, bleached white and brilliant in the sun. I squint—from this far away, I can see tiny shapes moving along the Wall, the walkers doing their due diligence. From here, I can't pick out features.

Behind me, Finn is still moving. Getting ready.

Apparently, that means changing into clean clothes and washing his face.

"We're wasting time," I grumble.

"Getting tossed in Q will waste more. So do what I said."

I grit my teeth. I hate that he's right. That we're waiting instead of rushing in, that rushing in won't save anything or anyone.

I want Collin. Being separated from him hums along my skin in an unnatural buzz—something I neither like nor am used to.

"Nurrin," Finn snaps, and I stand, spilling from my seat to push past him. I glare at the outfit he's laid out for me. It's better—barely—than the dresses he's put me in before, but it's still not what I'd like to wear.

Silk skirts and corsets, skinny jeans and shirts that leave me half exposed—none of it makes sense to me. I have always been most comfortable in zom gear and Collin's workout leathers. That isn't an option now. I have a part to play, and Finn is adamant that I play it well.

I dress quickly and pull my hair up into a tight pony tail and dab on some makeup.

When I step out of the bathroom, I go still, staring at him. He's hunched over a map, something very weary and broken about the way he stands there. It makes my heart twist a little.

Which is insane.

Finn doesn't get tenderness—he wouldn't want it even if I were inclined to give it to him. He's a heartless bastard.

And I hate him.

Sometimes it's hard to remember that. Like now, when he's shadowed by fatigue and worry, when the lines of his tattoos are stark against his tense skin. It's hard to remember how much I loathed him in Hellspawn. Why I did.

"You did well, in the fight," I say abruptly. His gaze flicks up to mine, surprise in his eyes for a heartbeat before it's chased away by disdain.

"I don't need your sympathy or your pity, Nurrin."

"You don't *need* to be an ass," I answer crisply. He smirks, a tiny twitch of the lips. "Do you think he's there?" I nod at 9.

He shrugs, looking out over the Wide Open to where it waits. "Maybe. We'll start in the morgue, see if they have Containment. Rule that out as quickly as possible."

I nod, my chest tightening. "Will the Aldermen help us?" *You*. That is the subtext of my question, and he grins over at me, reading it clearly. It's mocking, and I bristle, wanting to smack the look off his face.

I wish I had fought, earlier. Maybe it would have helped this unbearable tension.

"Always with the fucking questions."

I shrug, and he slides into the driver seat. I notice that he ignores my question completely as he puts the ZTNK into gear, and we lurch down the road toward whatever 9 holds for us.

Chapter 11. Old Habits

The Walkers look the same. The Walls look the same. Even the stupid weapons and the stupid gates look the same.

But this time, flashing a cool smile and a name doesn't earn Finn any special privileges. This time, the Walkers eye us with cautious distrust. Even when Finn clears the ZTNK and we pass our blood tests—and that will never get old, will it?—there is something cautious about them.

"What's your business in 9?" one asks. He's decorated—clearly their leader. I hide my smile at the way he stands there, his hands resting lightly on the hilt of his knives, his posture loose and unconcerned.

Two harmless Haven travelers, divested of their weapons, their blood tests clean.

That's what he sees—all he sees. Finn dressed us well for this part, with his too-polished clothes and insistence that I dress up.

We've made an impression, all right.

They're idiots, comfortable because they think we're no threat. That, more than anything, convinces me that they have no idea who Finn is.

No one could know Finn O'Malley and think he's anything less than a threat. He stands next to me, a relaxed stance. "Just a vacation with my fiancée. She's never been far from our haven."

"Why 9? Why now?" the leader asks.

"Her father had some business here, so we thought we'd deliver it for him. And my leave came now."

His gaze sharpens on us, and I shake my head. Finn slipped that in on purpose. "Leave. Are you a Walker?"

"Of Haven 29," Finn lies easily.

29 is to the east, along what used to be the Canadian border. It's far enough away that they won't bother to check our story. Finn *would* have

an easy story ready. I wonder, idly, if anything ever catches him unaware.

There's a brief discussion about our paperwork, which somehow got lost, and Finn loses his temper. It's amazing how quickly and well he can act.

"You have a hostel, don't you?" he finally demands.

The Walkers look disconcerted, and one says, "There's an empty room in the barracks, if you'd like to stay there."

Finn flicks a glance at me, and I make a face. A wealthy girl on her vacation wouldn't want to stay with soldiers in a smelly barrack. She'd be furious, and I know that's the part I have to play.

"I don't care where we go," I whine. "I just want to go to bed."

There's a beat of silence followed by a badly muffled laugh. My face flushes.

Finn's eyes seem to laugh at me before he shuts the emotion down and turns back to the Walkers. "We'll take it. Thank you."

"What of your transport?" the captain asks lazily. "Leaving a ZTNK like that is asking for it to be stolen."

For the first time, some of the idle disinterest slips from Finn, and I can see—*they* can see—the barely controlled violence simmering under the surface. "They are welcome to try," he says softly, expressionless.

The walkers go still, staring at him, as if they aren't really sure what to do. As if they suddenly realize the lamb is a wolf in sheep's clothing, and they let that into their Haven. A few exchange wild looks, and then Finn snaps his fingers at me and I snarl softly. His gaze darts to me. Without too much complaint, I go to his side, and we follow the Walker silently to the empty barrack that will be our home for the duration.

Chapter 12. Tiny Bed. Big Adjustments

The first thing I notice as we step into the room is that the bed is miniscule and narrow. An unfortunate looking mattress on a bare wire frame. A thing meant for utility and not comfort, and sure as hell not for sharing. I look away almost as quickly, my gaze colliding with Finn's. His gray eyes are roiling with emotion, but when mine meet them, he goes utterly blank.

Useful skill, that.

I'm anxious after the Walker abandons us, pacing the narrow room and avoiding thinking about what we'll do when night falls and exhaustion makes sleep unavoidable.

Then guilt slams into me. I'm worried about sleeping arrangements, while Collin is god knows where, enduring god knows what? How fucking petty can I get? I pause in my pacing, twisting to level a glare at Finn.

He meets it with a raised eyebrow. "What?"

“This is your fucking fault!” I snap.

“Do explain,” he drawls, his accent thickening a little—a sure sign he’s not as even tempered as he appears.

“Why the fuck didn’t you tell them your name? Smooth things along a little?”

“Can’t.”

I snort, “Your name has opened doors from 8 to the fucking Stronghold. Why is it different here?”

He gives me a flat stare, and I laugh, a little hysterical. “Oh, forgive me. You won’t answer a question like that. How silly of me to forget.”

“Don’t do that,” he says, annoyed.

“What?”

“That sarcastic bitchiness. It’s annoying as fuck.” I gape at him. “And you’re better than that.”

I can’t help the bitter laugh that wells in me, the one that sounds a little hysterical and on the very edge of shattering. I cut if off as Finn looks at me.

"It doesn't matter what happened in the other Havens, Nurrin. Here, my name will open no doors—I don't know anyone here. We'll get through this the way anyone would—by bribing our way and fighting like hell. Which we're very good at."

"We don't have *time,* for that," I snap shrilly.

"We also don't have a choice," he shoots back, his voice as bracing as a slap. "I don't have the time to coddle you. You have to get your shit together, or Collin is as good as dead."

The words are harsh and violent. They sting tears to my eyes, but they also jerk me up short. I shudder, knowing that he's right. I don't have the indulgence of wallowing and worry—not if there is even the slightest chance in hell of finding Collin alive. I take a deep breath, nod sharply to myself, and stare at him. Finn is watching me, his gray eyes caustic and demanding.

Exactly what I need him to be.

"What are we going to do?"

Something sparks in his eyes briefly—close to approval—before it's gone. "We'll listen to gossip, first. If that doesn't yield anything—check Q and Containment. Appeal to the Warden holders. If Collin and Dustin were here, they'll know, and they're accessible, even to us. See if we can get into the morgue."

I flinch, and he adds, "It's better to eliminate that possibility than to have it dangling over us the entire time we're in the Haven."

"And for now?"

"We'll rest. Get some sleep without the stress of the Wide Open and start fresh in the morning. I'll see if I can get some info from the Walkers—they might talk to me if they feel camaraderie."

I almost laugh at the idea of Finn O'Malley having camaraderie with anyone other than himself, or possibly Collin. But I have a feeling he can fake it, if he has to. There is very little that O'Malley can't do, if he has to.

"What will you do if Collin isn't here?"

Finn's eyes narrow a little. "You have yet to mention Dustin."

I stare at him, working through the words, trying to process them. Then I flush. "I want to get them both back. Obviously."

"It's not obvious," he says softly. "You want Collin back—from how often you've brought up Dustin, I wonder if you even remember he's what started this."

I flounder for something to say, but come up with nothing. Finn doesn't push further than that, just turns to the little bed where our bags are and rummages through them until he comes up with a few knives and two guns. The backup to replace the weapons the Walkers confiscated.

“I want mine back,” I say when he extends one to me. He nods, as close to a promise as I’ll get, and I take the standard Glock, tucking it into the empty holster on my hip.

Chapter 13. Twisted Priorities

I can't get Finn's subtle accusation out of my head. It wasn't an overt thing—Finn O'Malley doesn't need that. But it's a niggling presence in the back of my mind.

And it was there because it was the truth. I *had* forgotten Dustin.

Before Emilie Milan and the zombies and the horror show that life became—before I was born—people had different priorities. Life wasn't easily mapped out. Family was defined by more than blood. People fought with family and walked away from them completely, finding friends who would take their place. And it was common place, a normal occurrence.

Now, blood is all that matters—the blood that is shared, and the blood that is spilled.

Maybe that's why Dustin hasn't been my first concern, or even my second. Looking back now, I struggle to find the feelings I had for him. There is the warmth of something familiar and comfortable, a friend that's been a long standing fixture. But Dustin, for all that he's been in my life for almost ten years, isn't someone I've ever bled with or for. We had a safe life, a *good* life, in Hellspawn.

I haven't worried about him, because I've never needed to. Because he isn't my whole family and closest friend. He's Dustin. The goofy boy from downstairs who laughed and teased, who grew into a surrogate protector, and someone whose kisses could melt me like butter.

He was comfortable and steady, and I could easily have been happy with him, if the Haven hadn't fallen.

But it did.

And with the uncertainty I am now swimming in, there is no room for comfort— there is only the driving need to find Collin. It's a need that cramps in my belly and makes my mouth dry, my hands shake. It's a fear that that makes Finn at my side not only tolerable, but welcome.

Finn would move heaven and earth and face a horde alone to find Collin. Which means he is the only person I want helping me.

Chapter 14. Drifters

It's funny that I became accustomed to Finn's strange kind of influence so quickly. It was so effortless there in 18, it was easy to take it for granted. As natural as breathing, it was something that made doors open and annoyed me, but made things too easy, until it was gone.

There are no Aldermen scraping to meet us. There are no house calls from mysterious doctors in the middle of the night, no empty, dusty homes standing waiting for his return. There is no whispers of vice clubs and Undergrounds. We are met with closed doors and a few Walkers bored enough to entertain our questions.

By noon, I'm furious and more than a little scared. We know nothing more than we did yesterday.

"Calm down," Finn says under his breath, steering me down a market street. The Haven natives watch us with thinly veiled curiosity.

"Too long," I mutter, and his grip on my arm tightens a little. Not enough that I wince—just enough to get my attention and jerk me back to the necessity of keeping my calm.

"Talk to the women. I'll see if the men will tell me anything."

I shoot him a quick look—Finn isn't usually comfortable with a divide and conquer strategy. Tiny lines of stress bracket his eyes and lips. I nod.

The women are standoffish. They eye me warily as I separate from Finn, and I watch as they appraise us. Appraise him. There are more than a few admiring stares as we collectively watch his leather clad backside retreat.

Even I have to admit it's a helluva nice ass.

"Is he attached?" A girl to my left asks. She's pretty, just shy of the unhealthy side of thin, with short cropped black hair and the outline of a gun at her left hip. She's got enough innocence mixed with *don't fuck with me* to make her interesting.

Finn would like her. As much as he likes anyone.

I want to claw her eyes out. Instead, I shrug lightly. "I think he needs information."

A few women turn to look at me, their gazes harsher than they had been on Finn. Of course. Women are our own worst critics.

"What kind of information?"

I hesitate—Finn built our cover story, and I should probably stick to it. But I know what hook to dangle to get these women to help me. I nod at Finn. "My brother is his partner. He disappeared about a week ago—left behind a code that pointed us here. He was with my boyfriend. We're trying to find them."

The girl frowns a little. "We don't get a lot of visitors to the Haven."

"Then these two would make an impression," I say with a thin smile. I'm struggling to hold my temper when what I want to do is smack her and demand answers. Not that she would even have them.

"I don't know much. My brother is a Walker and said two refugees arrived three days ago. They were sent to Containment. You might want to try there."

I give her what might be a friendly smile and turn away. "O'Malley," I yell. His head lifts from where he's been talking to a Walker. His eyebrow goes up, and I nod. He doesn't say anything to the Walker, just stalks to me and matches my step as we leave the market behind.

Chapter 15. Containment

When the zombies took over the Wide Open, Havens were thrown up across the country as fast as they could be fortified. There was no rhyme or reason to it—they were numbered as they went into operation, scattered across the Midwest and past the mountains. There were even a few built in Canada.

Mexico was a black hole of death and infection—no one, not even the Mexicans, fought for it. They retreated to our cities, and when the plague found them there, they fell back into our Havens.

The first time a refugee convoy dumped evac citizens, it was at Haven 3, on a deserted plain in Kansas. It was the perfect place for a Haven, surrounded by farm land, self-sufficient, with enough excess crops to send to neighboring Havens.

It would have been a good place. In a time when there were *no* good places.

Except that in the chaos of the evac dump, a contact infection slipped in. Those days, there were no blood tests. There was nothing but the knowledge that the infects were in the Wide Open and the walls needed to be secure.

They escorted everyone inside and settled them into their new homes, and for the first time in months, everyone let out the breath they had been holding. Here, they were safe.

Here, they would live.

Three weeks later, a second convoy arrived with an evac dump. The Haven walls were unmanned, and black smoke rose behind the walls. The stench of death filled the air for miles. The contact infection that was carried in by that poor evac victim had gone live, infecting her. She, in turn, had infected the Haven.

Despite the perfection of the location, 3 was abandoned.

Blood tests were developed. Quarantine for anyone showing all three signs or exposed to a live infection. Containment for people who weren't infected, but were potentially a risk to the Haven, although some Havens skipped it in favor of Quarantine.

People bitch, quietly. It takes little provocation and absolutely no proof or justification to end up in Q or Containment, and spending three weeks in either is no one's idea of a picnic.

But it is a necessary evil, a part of the world we live in.

We approach the squat, square building, and Finn glances at me. "You can wait outside."

I don't even bother dignifying that with a response, just roll my eyes and keep walking toward the building. The stench of unwashed bodies and human waste slaps me in the face, making my eyes water, when I open the door. Finn makes a disgusted noise and props the door open. There are three Walker recruits sitting on either side of a triangular desk, so each was facing an open air, barred cells. They look bored, only mildly interested to see us standing in their doorway.

“Fucking amateurs,” Finn mutters, low enough that I hear it but they can’t. I agree with him, privately.

They aren't watching the Contained, and the shatter proof glass to Q is thick with grime and the viscous slog of infection.

This isn't a holding place to prove you are clean. This is a death sentence. My stomach lurches unpleasantly, and I falter in the doorway. I don't want to go in. Don't want to find my brother here. Something in me rebels at the mere possibility of it.

Finn has no such inhibitions. He strides in, ignoring the recruits completely as he walks to the first cage.

"Oi! You can't be here," one of the recruits says, his voice sharply disbelieving.

Finn doesn't bother to look at him, surveying the holding cells impatiently. Which means it's my job to make nice with the men with guns. I give the back of Finn's head a dirty look and fix a smile on my face as I stroll to the Walkers. The first one glares at me. "What the hell does he think he's doing?"

"We're looking for my brother. He came this way a few days ago, and we thought Containment would be a good place to start."

Amusement in their eyes. “If your brother is here, he’s as good as dead.”

Fear seizes my chest, and I can’t breathe.

“Containment isn’t a death sentence,” I choke out. The recruits relax—my fear makes me less of a threat, more someone they can victimize and control.

They have no fucking clue.

“In 9, that’s exactly what it is.”

I hear Finn’s low curse then the solid beat of his boots as he stalks away from the barred cells. His presence is heavy at my back, throwing waves of anger and violence. I shudder, and only a concentrated force of will keeps me from stepping away.

"I've been here now for almost twenty four hours," he says, his voice low and even. "I'm tired, I'm hungry, and I'm pissed. Now, you aren't responsible for the welcome we've received in 9—but you are here now, and you are responsible for Containment. Which is a fucking joke. So you get to answer my questions."

"Go fuck yourself," one of the Walkers snaps.

I shiver. It's the wrong thing to say. I can feel it in the stillness of Finn, in the sudden spike of tension—a kind of waiting violence, just needing direction. I smile. "You idiot," I breathe.

There is a flicker of confusion, and then a gun resting on my shoulder, pointing past my face, unwavering on the recruits. "I could. Or I could shoot you and go ask someone else questions. You can answer, or you can bleed. I don't particularly care which."

"I'm a Walker—shooting me is a federal offense." Shooting a recruit probably won't be as frowned upon as a full-fledged Walker, but the point is there.

"Yep."

There's a moment of hesitation before the click of the safety on Finn's gun. The Walker's eyes gets very big, and I sigh. "Just tell him. Have any refugees come to 9 in the past week?"

"Three," the recruit grits out. There is murder in his eyes, and only a strong sense of self-preservation is making him talk.

I don't frankly care—so long as he does.

"When?"

"Two days ago—three stumbled in. One hit the morgue a few hours later. I don't know what happened to the others."

"They left," one of the other says. "Serg said they were headed to The Stronghold."

Fear makes me move without thinking, twisting to give Finn a startled look.

And that's when the recruits act. I feel a sharp jerk, and Finn's eyes widen a half second before I'm jerked backward, out of his space and into the grip of the other men.

So stupid. So fucking stupid to forget for even a second that Finn wasn't the only danger. I go limp in their grip, and the quiet one, the third I hadn't been paying attention to because he hadn't spoken—*so fucking stupid*—has moved, jerking me away from the safety of Finn's orbit. I feel the metal of a knife pressed against my throat, and I go still.

"I don't have time for this," Finn mutters. His gaze darts from the knife to me to the Walker behind me. Rage flares, darkening his gray eyes for a moment, and then he shifts, his gun dropping slightly. I have just a half second to brace myself before he shoots. The recruit to my left, the first one to challenge us, screams, almost hitting the ground. Bits of blood and bone spray me as the bullet flies out the back of his leg. I grimace, glancing at my tight white shirt.

This is why you don't wear white. Ever. Someone is bound to get themselves shot, and you end up wearing it.

"You just signed her death sentence, man," the recruit holding me says, fury rippling in his voice.

"That's a flesh wound. Let her go, and I won't kill him," Finn says, almost bored.

I'm going to strangle him. When this is over and I don't have a fucking machete held to my throat—I'll strangle him. Antagonizing the people holding me by the throat...bastard.

"Do you have any veterans from the war?"

His grip on me loosens a little, curiosity piqued by the question. "Of course. Warden Ansliey. Every Haven has a few veterans. Why?"

"Get him down here. Tell him you have someone who would like talk to him."

"Why?"

Anger spasms across his face, and I think maybe he isn't as bored and blasé about this as he appears. "Tell him to come. Tell him one of the Thrasher's squad has a few questions."

There's a beat of hesitation, and I feel the knife shift a little lower, then up, nicking into my skin. I hiss, and Finn tenses, impossibly. "Tell him that—if he refuses to see me, you can do whatever the hell you want to either of us. But you tell him that, and if he'll see us, you let us go. And I won't shoot all of you."

The Walker hesitates—I can tell that he doesn't want to. He wants this settled now, with blood, for making him look bad. The one who was shot wheezes slightly at my left. The knife slides higher, and Finn hisses, watching it. My skin feels raw. Something tickles along it, and I realize belatedly that it's blood—he cut me.

"Don't," Finn murmurs. "Don't make me kill you."

The knife tightens again, and I gasp as pain flares hot at my neck. And then he relaxes and it drops down, bloody, at his side. I sag forward, and Finn catches me, his hands hard and impersonal as he pulls me away from the Walkers. This isn't about me, or that I'm bleeding. He shoves me behind him, without actually looking at me, and the Walker smirks, watching.

I flush. Fuck. Can he make things any more obvious? He all but pissed on me to mark his territory. Which would be less fucking annoying if he weren't Finn O'Malley.

He's a necessary evil, someone to help me find Collin. He is something I can't avoid. But in moments like this, I want to—I want to stab him with his own stupid sword and walk away from him forever.

How the hell did Collin ever put up with this asshat's behavior for so long?

The Walker is talking into the Haven comm, a radio that links the various wardens and important places in a Haven, his tone grumpy. He hangs up abruptly and glares at us, like we've done something specifically to annoy him while we stood waiting in silence.

I suppose since Finn did shoot his friend, he might just be grumpy in general.

"Ansliey is on his way," he announces, his lips tightening.

Finn doesn't react, doesn't do anything but lean farther away from them, into my space.

"Who the fuck is this guy?" the recruit demands of his superior, and the other man looks up. I see his name, now. Emerson. The one who almost slit my throat is named Emerson.

Why does that make my stomach twist, where his knife against my skin hadn't?

Finn ignores the question, but pulls a rag from the bag holding his spare ammo and tosses it to me. I stare at him darkly then wipe the blood away, wincing when the wound pulls unpleasantly. My stomach dips uneasily, and I swallow hard.

I'm not sick. I can't fucking afford to be sick right now. Not in a Haven like this, where Containment is a death sentence. This is nerves.

I shove the rag into a pocket and look up. Into his eyes, which are too steady and intense on mine. I suppress a shudder and look away.

Chapter 16. The Thrasher's Reach

Warden Ansliey is not what I expect. He's wiry and in his mid-thirties, with a thick head of bushy hair, bright blue eyes, and no nonsense attitude. His gaze sweeps over the entire scene as he stands in the doorway of Containment, ticking off the relevant details. Then he dismisses us entirely, focusing on the three recruits.

"What the hell is this?" he snaps. They glance around uneasily. "Containment is a safe place to wait, you idiots. It is not supposed to be a live infection—this is a hazard to the whole damn Haven. Does your commander know this shit hole looks like this? You know what—don't answer that. I'll take care of your commander. You get some fucking repellant and get this place cleaned. I'll be back with the Aldermen in two days—I've ignored this long enough. It'll be clean, or you can take your chances in Q."

The Walkers are staring, eyes slightly glassed. I bite the inside of my lip to keep from laughing. Serves them right, the arrogant little shitheads.

"Sir," Emerson starts, and Ansliey glares at him. Emerson pales and swallows hard. Goes quiet.

"You two," the Warden snaps, "with me."

"Sir!" Emerson interjects again, "he shot Halvers."

Ansliey glances at the Walker still on the ground. His gaze flicks over me, lingering on my throat, and then he shrugs. "You attacked his Thrasher. What the hell did you expect?"

I don't know what that means. From the confused looks on the Walker's faces, they don't either. But it *does* mean something.

"Come on," Ansliey grunts, turning away from the Walkers without bothering to speak to them again. He doesn't wait to see if we follow, just strides out to his Jeep, an open top thing with no defenses built in.

Either this man is a lot of talk who never wanders past the Walls, or he's a crazy as he seems.

I'm betting on the latter.

Ansliey has the Jeep on, the roar of it drowning out all sound as we approach. Finn grips my wrist, gives it a sharp tug, and I look at him. There is worry in his eyes, and he leans into me, his lips feathering against my ear as he whispers, "No questions, Nurrin. I don't know or trust him."

I smirk. "You don't trust anyone, O'Malley. That's half your problem."

Something flickers in his eyes, and he leans closer. "What's the other half, little girl?"

"You're too uptight. You need to get laid."

His hands find my hips, his grip tight.

It's not the same as the grip Emerson had—there is nothing about it that is hostile. But it is there, a solid grip that pulls me against his body, and I hiss as he rocks his hips into me, his cock nudging my ass. Then he lifts me up, setting me into the truck, and I look back at him, see the laughter in his eyes. I can feel him, his touch on every inch of my skin, and I hate that I like it. I hate that some stupid female part of me wants more of it.

I jerk away and settle into my seat. Ansliey is watching me in the rearview mirror, and my chin comes up, almost daring him to say something to me. His lips twitch and he shakes his head, but he keeps his comments to himself.

Finn swings into the passenger seat, and Ansliey eyes him briefly. "You're young to have fought for the Thrasher."

"Which should tell you something, if you think about it," Finn says evenly.

Ansliey grunts and shoves the Jeep into gear. I bite down on my questions—I won't get answers, and if I push, Finn will shut me out completely. Better to pretend I don't care and pick up what I can from listening.

The Warden drives through the Haven without talking, and I take it in quietly. The typical Haven is ten square miles—they started smaller than that, of course. Prisons and schools that were barricaded. But as time and necessity demanded, the Walls were pushed out to make way for factories, shops, schools, and farms. Until a whole world could be coalesced into one small square of land.

It feels familiar, while still being incredibly foreign. Like looking at home through a distorted lens. The orchards are replaced with crop fields, acres of wheat and corn and neat rows of soy and beans. A solitary track to the side, with an array of work-out machines in the center. Three Walkers jog around it.

The apartment complex is squat and greAlways always with the questionsy, not the tall building I lived in.

This Haven is so similar to home, and yet so different. And it reminds me, painfully, that I don't have a home anymore. That 8 belongs to the infects now. I'm alone and Havenless.

Tears sting my eyes, and I turn my face into the wind, hoping to hide them there. The very last thing I want is for Finn to catch me crying.

He doesn't respect weakness.

The thought startles me. Because there was a time when I don't care at all what Finn respected. Somehow, between Hellspawn falling and my brother going missing, that has changed, and I'm not sure how to feel about it.

The Jeep lurches to a stop. We sit still and silent for a few heartbeats, staring at the little cabin. It's nestled against the east Wall, with a small patch of grass converted into a personal garden.

There are no houses or businesses near it—the Warden apparently likes his privacy.

"Come on in. Your girl looks like she could use some time to clean up. We'll talk."

Finn nods, and I trail the two wary men into the house. It's neat, almost fanatically so, with a sparseness that makes me worry about the man. There are no knickknacks, no personalization. It is as sterile and untouched as Finn's home in 18.

This, I realize abruptly, isn't a home. It's a place to sleep and keep weapons. But the Warden isn't comfortable here—he moves through the space with a kind of awkwardness that says it's not a safe place.

And how terribly sad is that?

"Bathroom is through there, if you'd like to clean up," he says, pointing. "Unless you'd rather she stay put." Blue eyes flick to Finn briefly then back to me. He's being too solicitous, too careful around me. I tense—does he know I'm a First? He can't know that, not after ten minutes. I step closer to Finn, and Ansliey relaxes. "So she is your Thrasher."

I go still.

"She's under my protection. If you want to call her that, by all means, do. But she isn't who you think."

"What is one of the Thrasher's men doing this far south? I heard you were all given appointments in 1 after that last battle in New York."

"We were. I turned mine down. If you know anything about that battle, you'll know none of us deserved a promotion."

Something flickers across Ansliey's face, and his voice tips toward apologetic. "No one knew what to believe about that offensive, sir."

I can't hold back my laughter at that, and both men glance at me. "You're a Warden, and you're calling him 'sir?' In what world does that make sense?"

Ansliey smiles. "In a world where he served under the Brown Thrasher. No one who fought for her deserves less than my honor and respect."

I slide a glance at Finn. His hands are deep in his pockets, and a blank expression has settled over his face. "I thought you said your name wouldn't open doors here," I say, a little bitchy.

He shrugs slightly. "It didn't."

No. It didn't—his past did. How much does that bother him? From the tight grip he's got on himself and his emotions, more than I know.

"What can I do for you?" Ansliey says, picking up on the tension and changing the subject.

"First aid kit?"

Ansliey grabs it from the kitchen, and Finn tugs me to the table, pushing me down with my head tilted back as he inspects the wound on my neck. I keep my eyes trained on the ceiling as his fingers move with practiced precision over my wound. When he rubs it roughly with an alcohol swab, I hiss and look at him.

His face is blank as he works, but his eyes—his eyes are hot and furious. I shiver, and he meets my gaze, all of that emotion there for me to see.

And then it's gone, shut carefully away as he finishes cleaning my neck. I keep my gaze averted, and when he tapes the last gauze on and steps away, I mutter a quick thanks and straighten, moving away from him.

His gaze follows me, seeming to mock me. I ignore him and focus on Ansliey, who is watching us with a bemused look.

"What can you tell us of recent Haven arrivals?" Finn says abruptly.

"Three arrived a few days back. In pretty bad shape—we've been seeing a lot of refugees recently, more than we have in the past decade. I don't know where they came from—the Priest met with the Aldermen before they left again."

Finn frowns. "They were with a Priest? Of the Order?"

Ansliey nods. "Arrived together. The Priest and a sick one, in a truck. The other was on a bike."

My heart drops. Why the hell is Collin keeping company with a priest? What about that makes any sense at all? I open my mouth to say something, but Finn speaks quickly, cutting me off. "Did they go anywhere? Besides the Aldermen—did they meet with anyone, or indicate where they were headed?"

"The Stronghold. The Priest was pretty vocal about that being their destination." He hesitates, and then, "Come on. I'll take you where they were."

Chapter 17. The End of Hope

My head is swimming. Because it's too hot in the south. Because I'm exhausted and can't rest. Because my stomach still won't settle and my throat itches and stings when sweat slides down and catches on the sliced skin.

Or, maybe, because of where we're sitting.

The Jeep engine ticks quietly as it cools, but none of us have moved. None have spoken.

A lot of things change from one Haven to the next. They have to, to become distinctive and someplace people can call home. It's necessity as much as desire.

Two things don't change—the Walls—they are always tall and wide and white. And the Morgue. It is always next to the armory, patrolled by Walkers, and painted black.

I stare at the black building, panic building in my chest. A building of the dead, and they were here—why the hell were they here, what is Ansliey thinking, I can't do this, can't go in there, it's dangerous…

"Nurrin," Finn snaps, and I realize it's not the first time he's said my name. I shift in my seat. Take a deep breath. I can taste decay and death on my tongue, and it makes me want to gag. I shake my head and swallow hard. Shove the door open and almost fall out of the truck.

I can do this. I have to do this—whatever is inside, I have to face it.

Finn catches my arm as I start toward the morgue, staring down at me. I can see it in his eyes—I don't have to do this. I could let him.

Except that I can't. I have to be able to face this, or I'll be paralyzed. I have to see what's inside, even if it destroys me.

His lips thin and he lets go of me. For a second, I sway, but he doesn't reach for me. Doesn't help me get my feet under me. Just waits patiently as I do.

For some reason, he believes in me, and that means so much to me. More than Finn O'Malley should. I close my eyes and take a deep breath, then step forward. Ansliey trails us up the wide steps, stepping forward to speak to the morgue attendant as we enter. I twitch impatiently, and then we're moving again. I follow the morgue attendant down a long hallway, and then he opens the door. A stench of death slaps me, and at my side, Finn curses. Ansliey mutters something, but I can't hear him. I barely feel it as Finn presses a mask into my hand.

I can't feel it, and I can't see anything but the body lying on the table in front of me.

I don't know him—he's a stranger, younger than me. Maybe ten. Blond hair, feather fine, falls on the table in a long sheet. Blue eyes stare blankly at the ceiling. There is very little evidence of what killed him—faint bruising around his eyes and a redness to his mouth that suggests a contact infection.

And a neat hole in the center of his forehead, a gunshot directly to the brain.

My stomach twists, unexpectedly heaving, and I swallow, hard, struggling to keep the bile in my stomach.

Finn twitches at my side, and I shift past him, moving down the line of tables.

Haven 9 is small. They don't have many dead at any one time. Going through the morgue is quick, and as I near the back—only three tables from the last—my breath eases. They aren't here.

I look away from the end of the room, at the body on the table. And scream.

Chapter 18. The Grief of Permanence and Promise of Hope

The thing about the apocalypse is that it made life fragile. Life always was, but for those who had lived before, death was not an everyday occurrence. It was a tragedy, something that was actively feared. It was people's greatest fear.

And then, death became complicated, because it became less than permanent.

People survived because of hope. It wasn't the weapons or the army, it wasn't the walls of the Havens or the medicines pumped out by the drug companies working to fight their own creation. It was hope. That simple.

That insidious.

Hope that one day, death would be simple again. Hope that it would change. That the dead could be cured—that the world could be cured.

Everyone has a moment. That defining, life-altering moment when everything hinges on hope.

It can kill people, to see it dashed. I've seen it before, in the Haven, and after.

You never know how you will face the end of hope. Until you have no choice but to face it.

Chapter 19. Found and Lost

I've lost people. You can't survive in this world for twenty years without having lost people. But seeing him, lying there, a tiny round hole in his forehead—it's different. Different from when Mom died, eight years ago.

Different from watching Hellspawn fall or the parade of deaths on Day Three every year.

I scream again, but this time, there is no strength behind it, or in me. My bones go limp, and I hit the ground. I close my eyes, willing it away, the vision.

Dustin looks nothing like the boy who woke in my bed the day Hellspawn fell. His skin is ravaged and gray with infection, his green eyes filmed with it. The muscles in his face have begun to sag. The neat hole in his forehead is rimmed with black, a sure sign the infection was moving too fast.

I take all of the details in, but nothing makes sense. Nothing is sinking in.

Dustin is here. Dustin is dead. Collin—

"*Collin,*" I gasp and lurch forward.

Hard hands catch me, tug me up. I meet gray eyes and see the understanding there. And the demand. Tears well in my eyes, and I gasp, struggling to keep from falling apart. "Collin," I whimper, my brother's name a plea.

Finn ignores me and motions to Ansliey. "Take her to the Jeep," he orders. The Warden doesn't protest, just takes my arm gently and leads me out as Finn talks to the morgue attendant. I can almost taste the questions on the back of my tongue. Distantly, I want to go back and demand to be included.

"Who was he?" Ansliey asks, the question a gentle intrusion. I blink at the Warden, the one I never expected.

"Who is the Thrasher?"

His eyebrows go up. But he doesn't hesitate to answer, maybe because he just watched me crumple. "Kelsey Buchman. The daughter of President Buchman—she led several key assaults in the Battle for the East."

The world spins. My gut heaves, and everything that still made sense—which wasn't much—disappears.

Who the fuck *is* he?

Chapter 20. The Impossibility of Breaking

Ansliey doesn't push as we wait for Finn. Maybe because after his little revelation, I retreat into silence, staring at the sky until sunspots dance in my eyes and my head spins. Maybe because just when he does gather the nerve to speak, Finn emerges from the morgue. I'm aware of him, but I don't turn to look at him. I just stare at the sun, hoping that it will burn out the image of my dead lover.

"Can you take us to the barracks? I need to drop her off, and then I want to talk to the Aldermen," Finn says.

"Don't bother. I'm going with you," I say, not moving.

"No."

That does get a reaction. "Excuse me?"

"You need to go and get a hold of yourself," he says dismissively.

Grief gives away to rage so quickly I can't process it. I can only lean forward, into Finn's face, and hiss, "He was mine. My lover. You have no right to say what I need now that he's dead. Collin? He's mine. My brother. Do you think for a minute he's thinking about you, lost out there? Go fuck yourself, O'Malley."

"He is," Finn murmurs, a smirk turning his lips. It enrages me, and I jerk back, ready to smack him. He catches my hand before it can connect, uses it to jerk me forward. "He's thinking about me, Nurrin," he whispers, so close I can feel the heat of his breath on my lips, "because he knows I will keep you alive. Remember that."

Then he releases me, so abruptly I fall backward in my seat. I can see Ansliey watching us with wide, confused eyes, and I wonder what he thinks of this.

If he's still under some delusion that I mean anything to Finn O'Malley.

I don't. I am merely a promise he is fulfilling.

"To the Aldermen, then," Finn says, soft and even. I ignore him and focus on the sky again as the Jeep rumbles to life.

We drive in cautious silence. Something about Finn's insistence on seeing the Aldermen bothers me—I want to confront him about it, but I can't.

Not with Ansliey listening and Finn's lips a thin angry line.

Not with the knowledge of who Kelsey is.

When we stop, I don't bother looking around. I can't see past the sunspots. Even if I could, all I would see is Dustin. No need to look around for that. I drop out of the truck and tug my shirt into place. I can feel them watching me, and it makes my chin come up.

I refuse to let Finn fucking O'Malley see me break.

I stride to the steps of the Haven government building, taking the moment to shove the pain down, down deep where I can't feel it for now.

Later. On the road. When Finn isn't staring. When Collin is safe. Then I can shatter into the grief clawing at me. But for now—now I let it simmer and embrace the anger just beyond it.

Because anger is easier. So much easier than grief will ever be.

Chapter 21. Heedless Warnings

The Aldermen are gathered around a large round table, arguing over a report that looks like it's seen better days. When I enter through the open door, they don't even notice. I hesitate there, a lifetime of respect for the people who run a Haven keeping me from interrupting.

Finn apparently has no such reservations. He slides past me, directly to the table. Refusing to be left behind, I move to flank him as Ansliey circles the table to stand near a curly haired woman. Her eyes narrow as they assess us. In any other circumstance, the lingering glance at Finn would bother me, but then her gaze darts to me. I don't know what she sees, but she pales.

"What can we do for you?" she asks. Whatever she's feeling, her voice is steady and strong.

Bonus points for her.

"We're just passing through, Alderman. But we wanted to warn you—the Havens are being attacked."

"We heard a little." She makes a face. "Or maybe it would be better to say we haven't heard. From several Havens. I take it you have some theories or information?"

"ERI-Milan has mutated. It's the only explanation. Without a scientist or lab, we can't really say much more than that, but the disease has changed, and because it has, the zombies have. The hordes are bigger, and they're working together—we haven't seen numbers like this since the change."

"But we're safe behind the Walls."

"No. I don't think we are. That's the problem—we've gotten comfortable behind the Walls, and now things are changing and we aren't. You need to be willing to change, or this Haven will fall, just like 8 and 18."

"We haven't heard 18 fell," the curly haired woman says sharply. "Who the hell are you?"

"Cora, this is Finn O'Malley. Walker in Haven 8 and a veteran of the East."

Her eyes narrow, and she snorts dismissively. "How old are you, O'Malley? What on earth do you think you know about something you can barely remember happening?"

Disgust sours my stomach. "He didn't have to come here. He didn't have to give you any warning—we're leaving, and he could have gone and let the whole damn Haven take its chances with the Horde. But we took the time, and we're here. And you'll dismiss it just because you think he's too young?" My voice is thick with disbelief and a little mocking—maybe because I'm not trying to keep it from seeping through. "That's not just shortsighted, it's stupid and reckless."

I turn to Finn. "You've given them the stupid warning. It's time to go."

Finn doesn't say anything as I turn on my heel and stalk out. Maybe he has something left to say to the idiots who run this Haven, but I'm done.

I'm leaving. Collin is out there, with a priest of all fucking things. And I'll do whatever it takes to get him back.

Chapter 22. Impossibly Surreal

The room feels suffocating small. Even more so than it did last night, when all we had was a tiny bed to share—Finn ended up sprawling on the end, while I curled in the dirty corner, half sitting.

Now it feels half that size, and every move he makes, every brush of fabric over his skin, rubs at exposed nerves.

Maybe it's because my grief is welling up so big it will make even this tiny room smaller. Can a feeling eclipse space, shrink it to something that is insignificant and negligible?

Because right now, it feels like it can.

"The Aldermen were startled by how rude you are," he says. I swallow hard and jerk at the lacing of my corset top. Is that really what he wants to talk about?

"Because if I had been a polite little windup doll, you would have been the same?

You were about five seconds from shooting one of them."

Oh look at that. I *can* sound normal, even when grief is choking me.

"I have the right to be a bastard—I've lived long enough and killed enough that no one can say a damn thing."

"Is that what it is? Killing gives us rights?"

He goes still and silent, and I shake my head, jerking the corset off abruptly. The lacings sting against my skin, and then it's gone and I can breathe. "I think death should earn me something. Watching my best friend dead on a morgue table— "

"What the fuck are you doing?"

Something about his voice warns me to stop, that this is dangerous. But dangerous seems like a brilliant idea right now. I twist to face him. "I'm falling apart. Do you have a problem with that?"

"Yes," he snaps.

I stalk to him and shove at his chest, furious. "Then go. Leave me the fuck alone, O'Malley. Go find someone who knows who the hell you are and gives a shit—I don't need you."

"You're better than this," he snarls, shoving back.

"He was my *lover,* you bastard," I scream.

His face spasms, and he shoves me into the wall. "He was a boy. A distraction. You deserve so much more than a paltry Haven boy."

"You have no idea what you're talking about," I hiss.

Finn's eyes flick down, and I realize, abruptly, that I'm in nothing but the skin tight pants and strapless bra.

"I know that you need someone as strong as you. Someone who won't be under some fucking delusion that you need protection."

"Dustin was strong," I whisper.

Finn laughs, his hands on my hips tightening, almost bruising. "Dustin wasn't what you need."

"How do you know?"

A mocking smile. "You walked away. When you find that one thing you can't live without—that person—losing them will destroy you. It won't be something you walk away from. Dustin was a distraction—a plaything. Nothing more."

I slap him, hard. And I don't know if it's because he has the gall to say that to me, or if it's because I hate him for being right. A smile ticks up the corner of his lips, and then he's kissing me.

And I don't push him away. I gasp under his lips, and he growls, a low noise that hits me, low, his fingers digging into my hip as his tongue sweeps into my mouth. It twists with mine then retreats, and I whimper. He catches the noise, sucks lightly on my lip and my tongue, and I can't—I can't breathe. I can't breathe and I don't even care.

His lips rip away from mine, and I whimper, terrified he'll step away. But he doesn't. His big hands come up and jerk my bra cups down.

I have a half second to think—bad idea—and then his fingers are on me, plucking at my nipples, and I groan, arching into him. His lips skim down my neck, nibbling, and I go limp against the wall, braced by the knee between my legs, and his body holding me up, his hands pinning me there.

He pinches my nipple, and I shudder, almost coming off the damn wall. Wet heat wraps around it. I swallow a scream. Every nerve comes alive as Finn traces my nipple then sucks gently.

He thrusts his knees against me, and I move, rubbing against him as he works me over. With every brush of his teeth, every pull of his mouth on my nipple, twist of his fingers, and thrust of his leg, everything in me coils tighter, until I can barely see, all I can do is feel. His hand leaves my nipple, and I almost scream, teetering on the edge. His hand catches mine, jerks it between us, to cup his erection. I gasp as he rocks into my touch. I open my eyes and look at him.

I expect him to be closed off, his eyes vacant or closed. Anything but what I see.

Finn is staring at me, his gaze hot and demanding, taking in every twitch of pleasure as his fingers caress me and his body rocks against mine. I can see the hunger in his eyes, and then he twists, and his knee hits me again, just right. I can't see anything as the orgasm hits me, hard. I shudder, pleasure sweeping over me in endless waves, and the world spins—it actually motherfucking spins.

When I can breath—when the tremors ease and I can move without twitching in remembered pleasure—I open my eyes to find myself on the bed. Finn has his back to me, his shoulders hunched as if expecting me to start screaming.

What just happened hits me, and I take a breath.

"Get dressed. We'll leave in the morning," he says.

I open my mouth, to ask where, to ask anything. And then I close it again, because there isn't anything to say.

I crawl off the bed and grab a t-shirt off the top of my bag. Finn is very careful to keep his back to me as I strip out of my bra and pants, redressing quickly in the new t-shirt.

My panties are wet. It's all I can think about as I curl in my corner of the bed. Finn flicks the light out, and the room is plunged into darkness and a new level of tension.

As I lie in the darkness and listen to Finn's steady breathing, I can smell the scent of sex. On me, and him, and the air. I flush and twist to get comfortable.

What will this strange partnership be like now? What the hell came over him, that he would do that? Is it that he's bored and I'm the only girl readily available? Finn hates me—I'm something he was saddled with, a burden he's carrying because of a loyalty to my brother. So what was this?

I don't have answers. As usual, with Finn, I only have a lot of unanswered questions.

And the unavoidable knowledge that no one—not Dustin—ever made me feel like that before.

Chapter 23. The Familiar Road

"I could come."

The words shift through the small room, and Finn pauses in the middle of shouldering his sword. Looks at Ansliey with curious and unsurprised eyes. "You are a Warden, sir. Leaving isn't really an option, especially since we have no idea when we'll be back this way."

Disappointment shadows the Warden's face, and I think I understand.

"They need you," I say softly. Finn stiffens. "The Haven is in danger—if you aren't here, it will fall. You're a war vet—you can help prevent that."

"Or I can go down with a dying Haven," he says, his voice bitter.

"You are their best chance for survival. Would you take that from the entire Haven?"

He snorts. "The Haven is run by politicians with little time for a war vet who is more crazy than he is cautious. They won't listen to me—and I'll let the Haven fall before I give the infects a chance at me."

Finn hesitates, and I look at him. He's ignored me all morning, ignored the tension that spikes whenever we brush against each other in the small room.

"Have a plan. You won't be able to save them all, but you might save a few and you'll have a better chance at getting out alive if you have a plan. Don't count on the gates—those will lock down as soon as the Horde gets close. Have another way out. Don't go to the Hatch—those will be death traps."

"Is that how you got out? When Hellspawn fell?"

Finn's lips thin, but he nods reluctantly. "Yeah. It is."

Ansliey frowns, clearly unhappy, but he nods.

And that quickly, we're done. We're ready to leave. Except...

"Dustin," I say softly. Both men turn to look at me, and I see the tension in Finn's face tighten, just a little. He doesn't like me asking about Dustin. Not even this little bit.

Well, fuck Finn and what he likes.

Ansliey's lips tip into a slight smile, and he pulls out a thin silver chain. A tiny vial swings from it, and tears cloud my eyes. I take a deep breath, determined to get through this meeting without breaking down like a little girl on her first day of school.

"I thought he seemed important to you. I can't give you everything—Haven procedures when we have a mutating virus."

I nod, and he hands me the thin chain. The little vial swirls and clouds with gray dust—not much at all, but so much more than I expected. "Thank you," I whisper, hugging him suddenly.

Ansliey goes stiff and startled, and then he relaxes into my embrace, patting my shoulder softly. "I'll see him buried, girl."

I nod and pull back, wiping my eyes quickly. I loop the thin chain over my head and let the cold vial settle against my skin, the ash inside swirling and slowly coming to rest.

It's a tiny memento, but it is more than I expected. It will be enough, because it has to be. I step away from the Warden, and Finn clears his throat. Tosses me my pack. And that fast, we're done—ready to leave once again.

Chapter 24. Destinations and Clues

We're in the ZTNK, pulling the truck behind us. I'm not sure if that's because Finn wants the versatility of an extra vehicle, or if he's too stubborn to leave it behind in a Haven we will likely never return to.

I move around the back of the RV, getting our bags stowed and changing out of the corset and into a loose practice shirt. A bag of weapons gets tossed between the driver and passenger seat and I grab two bottles of water from the RV's fridge before dropping into my seat and cross one leg under me, handing Finn a bottle of water silently before I flip open the book in my lap.

"What is that?"

It's a thin book I found in the barracks last night, when I couldn't sleep and slipped out.

I'm still a little surprised I was able to get past Finn without waking him. Or maybe it's just that he didn't care that I was leaving.

"Oral history of the Change."

He glances at it, and I hold it up. The title is very self-explanatory, but I elaborate anyway. "People who were in the Battle for the East, and who survived that first few years—these are some of their stories."

"Everyone has a story," he says dismissively.

I pin him with a hard stare. "Everyone does, but not everyone wants to talk about it. Unless you'd like to talk to me about the Thrasher? Because I can put this down, if so."

His gaze darts to mine, furious, and I smirk. "That's what I thought, O'Malley."

I turn back to my book. I don't really want to talk to Finn any more than he wants to talk to me, and I definitely don't want to remember the feel of his leg between mine, his mouth on me.

He opens his mouth, and for a moment, I think he'll talk. That he'll tell me one damn thing without me having to beg for it or fight it out on my own. Instead, he makes a face and focuses on the road. I stare at the page, the words blurring as my temper rises, and reach for the vial hanging between my breasts. I clench it, hard, and fight to even my temper. Flip to the next page and try to read these strangers' horror stories.

Ironic, that I will know more about them than I will about the man I've been traveling with for two weeks.

"Why do you suppose he went to the Stronghold?"

"What?" Finn says, distracted as we weave down the potholed road. Clearly 9 has priorities, and maintaining the roads in and out of it aren't high on the list. Maybe it's their proximity to the border.

"Collin and that priest. Why would he go with a priest to Vegas?"

"He didn't."

I jerk hard in my seat, twisting to look at Finn.

"There was another message. With the morgue attendant. He's not headed to the Stronghold—he's going to 6."

"Why there?"

"Why not?" Finn shrugs. "I don't really know, Nurrin. I'm just following the breadcrumbs and hoping we get to him before they run out. But what it does tell us is that he's alive—or he was three days ago."

That's true, a comforting truth. But maybe he isn't anymore. Maybe Finn is feeding me that line of hope because I'm crumbling and he can see through my shell and tell.

Whatever the reason, I'm grateful for it. I nod a little, blinking back the tears that are stinging my eyes. "So. Not the Stronghold?"

"Not this time. As much as I'm sure Omar would love to see us."

"What happened between you and Omar?" I ask, the question out before I can stop it.

Finn's grip on the steering wheel tightens, enough that the plastic creaks alarmingly. "What is the only thing that matters?" he asks, softly.

I don't have to question what he's talking about. "You will keep me alive and keep Collin alive."

Something flickers across his face, and then, "Omar betrayed me. He betrayed the mission. I can forgive a lot—but not that."

There's more to it—so much more, from the rage in his voice. But for once I'm not interested in pushing him.

"One day, you'll trust me enough to tell me some of what happened to you," I says softly. He looks at me, staring as we bump down the road, and I don't look away. Finn finally smirks, a mocking twitch of his lips before he turns back to the road. I let out the breath I'm holding and lean my head back on the seat.

"One day, little girl, you will have earned it."

Chapter 25. Another New Place

The trip to 6 is surprisingly uneventful. With a bed to crash on and plenty of food, we don't need to stop for much—once for gas at a fortified little station that sells us fresh, hot sandwiches, and then we're on our way again.

Moving is the safest way to be, in the Wide Open.

"What will we face in 6?" I ask.

Finn shrugs. "I don't know. I've never been there."

"So we won't be trusting your name to open doors?" I ask, flipping a page. I'm almost through with my little book, and feel like I'm no closer to knowing anything.

Certainly this book has nothing about the Thrasher and why she was so important in the East. The account I'm reading now is from a sailor on one of the last boats to make dock in New York before ERI-Milan mutated in Atlanta.

Finn ignores my question. Typical.

"Where are you from?" I ask abruptly. "Originally?"

Finn shoots me a startled look. "That is your burning question? Where I was born? What the hell does it matter? I'm here now. I've been here for over twenty years."

"One question," I grit. His eyebrows arch, and I shake my head. "I'm not pushing about Kelsey or Omar, or why the fuck every haven seems to know your name—all important things, by the way. I'm not demanding to know what's so important about Collin that you will do all of this to find him. I'm asking where you were born."

I stand and start to the back of the RV, unable to stomach him anymore. I pause. "You demand a lot of trust from me. A lot of tolerance for a ton of bullshit. You can't expect me to trust you without reservation if you won't give a little."

It's late that night—he let me sleep longer than I thought he would, maybe because I yelled at him. Although that's not typical behavior for Finn.

The ZTNK rumbles to a stop, and he calls back to me. "We're here."

I roll onto my back and stare at the ceiling for a long minute, trying to shake the fog of sleep, and process that we've arrived. The air is drifting in from Finn's open window, and it tastes wilder—bigger—than anything I've ever known. Distantly, I can hear a dull roar.

I roll from the bed and twist my shirt straight, then shamble up to the front and drop into the seat next to him.

He glances at me then back at the Haven. "We're just ourselves here. If Ansliey got in touch with them, it's too late to lie."

"But you won't be able help us by flaunting your name."

"Not here. But that was true of 9 as well," he reminds me. "And we still did fine."

I don't take the bait. Too much about Finn is pushing me too far. I need space from him, time to think. I need my brother, to remind me why I trust this enigmatic man.

Neither are options right now.

We roll up to the gate, and I stare at the wide white walls, reminding myself that Collin is why I'm doing this—any of it.

"Do you think he's still here?" I murmur.

Finn sighs. "I really hope so. But if he's not, we'll keep going. You know that, right?"

I bite my lip, and he reaches over.

His fingers are hot on my chin as he twists me to look at him, but gentle—softer than I expect from him. "We *will* keep going. Until we find him."

I stare into his eyes for a long heartbeat, longer than is really comfortable, and even though I don't have any reason to, I trust him.

Maybe Finn doesn't answer questions, but he doesn't lie either. It's an annoying trade off, but I'll take it.

The gate clatters open, and two Wall Walkers jog out, one assuming a defensive position while the other taps on Finn's window. He rolls it down and slips out our IDs.

The Walker frowns at them then glances up quickly, handing one card over his shoulder to his partner. The man glances at it and wordlessly retreats back to the gate.

"I thought you said you weren't known here?" I murmur.

Finn is frowning, watching the two Walkers. He doesn't respond to my comment. A few more Walkers clatter out of the gatehouse, slipping into the Wide Open, and neither of us misses the fact that they are heavily armed.

What the fuck is happening?

"You don't know me. Understand? You found me on the roadside, and we traveled together for a few days, but you don't have any past history with me and you have no idea who I am. Do you understand?" he says, voice low and urgent.

"No," I whisper, because I don't understand. And because I know one thing—Finn is the best chance I have of finding Collin.

His gaze flashes to mine, and I tilt my chin up, a silent challenge. "This is not a good time to decide to trust me, Nurrin," he growls, frustrated.

"I don't," I say. "But I need you."

I glance out the window instead of watching his reaction. The Walkers have circled the front of the truck, and they're all armed—with those guns pointed at us.

"Finn," I say, staring.

He curses, low and vicious, and leans across the bag of guns between us to murmur. "Take the wheel. Try not to be combative—I have no idea what's going on, but let's try not to get shot today. Okay?"

Without thinking, I reach for his hand. His grip on my fingers is tight, strong—it steadies me. He pushes the door open and releases me, sliding out while I wiggle into the driver's seat.

I can see the glances the Walkers are sliding toward me, but Finn is blocking me with his body. His tone is furious.

"Do you greet all visitors like this?"

"You'll need to be tested," the Walker says without answering his question. If he thinks that will put Finn off his stride, he knows nothing, no matter what he thinks.

Finn waits patiently as a medic scurries out, fixing him with a fierce glare before focusing on the needle stick. When she's done, she flicks her eyes to me. I can feel Finn's tension shoot up, even without him touching me, and I force an easy smile.

Clean tests are no one's idea of a good time, but I am clean, so it's nothing to be worried about. I extend my arm, and she jabs it, a little harder than necessary. I hiss a breath. Finn shifts. "Be careful."

The medic snorts. "I don't take orders from you, O'Malley. I never have."

Finn jerks back, and I shoot him a confused look.

For the first time, he looks just as lost as I am. And I realize something.

I trust him. I don't know what he hides or what will happen next. I don't know from one minute to the next how we'll get out of whatever mess we've found ourselves in. And I deal with that not knowing because I trust that *he* does. It's flawed, imperfect, and frustrating. But it works for us, and I am comfortable there.

This—this *not knowing,* with both of us lost, isn't a place I like to be. I didn't realize until it was jeopardized just how much I trust Finn's odd brand of handling things.

The medic straightens, handing me a swab of cotton to clean my arm. She gives me a look of loathing and stalks away. "She's clean. They both are. Strip him of his weapons."

Finn jerks, the crossbow coming up and leveling at the medic. "You might rethink that, sweetheart."

The medic laughs, a twisted noise. She hates him. I don't know why, but I know, deep down in my gut, that it's true. I twist to look at Finn, who still has her pinned with the crossbow.

He meets my gaze, and I can see what he wants—me to leave. Cut my losses and get the fuck out.

Idiot.

He's going to *hate* this.

I toss my knives out the window and watch them embed at Finn's feet. His gaze goes furious—so angry it makes me shiver. Even when I did something stupid and risked my life for his in 8, he has never looked at me with this much anger.

The medic smirks, turns to look at me, and says softly, "The rest."

"This gun is special," I tell her, ignoring Finn completely now. "You damage it at all, O'Malley will be the least of your concerns. Do you get me?"

"You aren't in the position to make demands. Sanders."

She nods abruptly, and the Walkers shift to point their guns at me. A gleeful smile twists her lips up, and I shake my head, leaning back to stare at her. "You aren't smart, are you?"

Anger colors her cheeks, but she doesn't lose her temper. Instead she cocks her head to the side and grins. "Take them. Both of them. I'll gather the panel."

She turns away without waiting to see if they will listen, trusting that her word will carry. Bitch. Finn steps into her space as she moves to skirt past him, and he murmurs, "If anything happens to her, I will bring down everything I have on you. Not this Haven. Not the Walkers—you. Do you have any idea what that means?"

Her gaze flicks to me, steely, then back to Finn. "I think the whole world knows what that means, O'Malley." She shakes off his grip and stalks away. The Walkers close in around us, and I move closer to Finn. He glares over at me. I shrug lightly.

"Let's go," one of the Walkers barks, and just like that, we're taken into custody.

Chapter 26. The End at the Beginning

Some things were irreparably changed after the zombies rose. A lot of things, if we're honest. Emilie is a name more known than some presidents, and—in some minds—as infamous as Hitler. The way of life, travel, education, our everyday sense of security—all of that vanished when Emilie died.

We didn't even realize it was over, not then. Not when the president deployed a thousand soldiers against the mob in Atlanta.

And the worst part is, that wasn't the end. That wasn't the beginning. Both moments in time were occupied by the same thing: the moment that ERI was commissioned and accepted for use. The first time a brilliant mind—and it was; only a very brilliant mind could conceive of a way to suppress emotions and pass it off as a good thing—happened along the idea and went to the lab to execute it.

Synthrix did one thing that for years was lauded as a life saver. A life changer.

They were right. It changed everything. And scientist have been working ever since to undo that damage.

Chapter 27. Detainment and Surprises

We're put in Containment. 6 was a prison before it was converted to a Haven, and even though it's been expanded to a sprawling Haven with miles of Walls, at its heart, it's still a prison with a prison mentality.

They march us into a tiny cell, and when they try to separate us, Finn goes icy and still, a hairsbreadth from danger. I clear my throat. "You are detaining two citizens who have no infection. We've broken no laws. I think you've pushed as far as you can without us losing our patience completely—we stay together."

They confer briefly, and the leader shrugs. "Caitlyn said nothing about separating them."

Once we're safely locked into the tiny cell, the Walkers fall back and watch us, talking softly amongst themselves.

"What the hell is going on?" I demand in a near whisper.

Finn flicks a glance at me. "Always with the fucking questions, Nurrin."

Jokes. The idiot has jokes, now, of all times. I roll my eyes and turn away, dropping onto the single narrow cot. It's creaky and hard as hell.

"I don't know. And I don't like not knowing. I wish you had listened to me and left."

"To do what, exactly? I can't find Collin without you." I say the words without bitterness. A first. A smirk tugs at his lips, and his eyes are all mocking when he says, "Don't get soft, Ren. Not now. Hold onto your anger."

I flush. The door opens, and we watch as the Walkers file out, leaving us alone.

Finn sighs, a weary noise, and slides down the wall, propping his hands on his knees. I mirror his pose on the cot, and we fall into silence—one I feel no need to break—as we wait.

They keep us waiting until the sun has dropped in the sky and hunger is gnawing at my stomach. The Walkers never return, and Finn is quiet. I'm bored out of my fucking skull, and I can't help the occasional glances I sneak his way. I can't help but watch the way his lips go soft as he leans his head back and lets the tension ease out of him.

I can't help but remember the feel of those lips. Goosebumps ripple along my skin, and I look away.

"I hated you, you know," I say, absently.

Finn breathes a laugh, all ironic acknowledgment. "I do recall that, yes. It's very easy to hate something we don't understand, Nurrin. And you have never understood my relationship with Collin."

"Explain it to me," I say. Not a challenge this time, but an invitation. He looks at me, expression unreadable. I hold my breath, waiting.

And the door opens, before he has the chance to say anything. Three Gray-robed priests glide into the room. I feel everything in me clench—a lifetime of knowing the Order is my worst enemy and greatest threat. I curl into a smaller ball, trying to make myself invisible as they stare.

At Finn. All of them are ignoring me. I frown, slowly uncurling, my feet falling to the ground as I straighten. What the hell is going on?

"I'm not terribly surprised you're here," one of the Priests says, a smile tickling his lips.

"Ah. So this is where the Grays settled. I didn't realize you made it to the ocean," Finn says, and I flick a glance at him.

"Let them out. I don't like discussing business through bars." The Gray looks at me, his eyes an unnervingly clear blue. "I apologize, ma'am."

He gives Finn a curious look. Finn has come to his feet, and he extends a hand, pulling me up. An arm wraps around my waist, and he tugs me into him. His lips brush my hair. “No names. Nothing to make them thing you are anything more than a traveling companion. Got it?”

I nod, and Finn straightens away from me. Smiles as the Blessed Order leads us from the room.

My mind is racing, and I grasp onto facts as I move alongside Finn. I have never seen a Gray Priest before. I know nothing about their sect within the Order. But the medic ordered our detainment, based on who we were rather than what we might be carrying into the haven.

And the Gray Priests are who she summoned. That alone tells me a lot, and it’s nothing I like.

Some havens are run by the Aldermen. Some are run by the Walkers and are militant. A very few are under the sway of 1 – but no one trusts the federal government after they bombed our own cities. The rest are given more to anarchy – to the people and their whims.

And the Order. The Order holds more Havens then I like to think of, but I have never heard of one so under their influence.

Places like this are the stuff of nightmares for people like me.

I've never been to one. Colin has done well all my life keeping me from safe the Order. Yet with Finn I've been close to them three times in only a few weeks. What on earth makes me continue to trust him?

They are divided into sects, even within their own religion. The Black Priests control their military arms. The Red control sacrifices and conversion. I know nothing about the Gray. Except that they know Finn.

"Do you know what this is about?" I ask.

Finn's lips thin. "No."

I want to tease him, if only to ease that worry line between his eyes. But now is hardly the time. Instead, I reach for his hand, squeezing it briefly. His eyebrows shoot up, and I smirk before I release him and we follow the Order in silence.

Chapter 28. Science and Religion

The room we follow the Grays into is brightly lit. Glass vials are neatly stacked, microscopes and lab equipment wiped down to a pristine shine. A few more gray-robed priests are in a corner, talking over a small sterile dish of something thick and black. Four men in white coats are clustered around the remains of an infect, a bloody gash down her face.

It's very clear, very quickly. The Gray Priests are scientists. Which is just fucking wonderful. Because fanaticism isn't nearly enough—nope. It needs to be paired with just enough knowledge to make you truly deadly.

"Finn O'Malley. I'll admit I didn't expect to see you here. We've never made a secret of the fact that we aren't fans of yours."

"I'm not sure I should care," he says, stepping away from me and closer to the lab equipment. There's a tablet with a display lit up, and I'm surprised that no one attempts to remove it. Finn glances it over. Shakes his head. “This premise is flawed.”

The Grays still conversing over the specimen stop talking and come to where their brothers stand. The white-coat scientists bristle. “Explain yourself.”

Finn tosses the tablet back down, and it clatters. “You are looking for a cure to ERI-Milan, strain 73. But that strain has already mutated. You're working from a corpse—it's not relevant anymore.”

“How the hell would you know?” the scientist snaps.

“Because he's Finn O'Malley,” one of the Grays interjects smoothly. “I believe, Dr. Levine, even you are aware of whose son he is.”

“Just because he's Sylvia Cragen's son doesn't mean he knows anything about the way her disease works.”

"No," Finn says softly. "Time and experience taught me how it worked. And it was not a disease. It was a cure."

The words are spinning around me, and some of the puzzle pieces of who he is fall into place.

Sylvia Cragen. Holy Jesus. This can't be real—it can't. I twist and stumble a few steps away, hitting my hip on a lab table. I can feel the Grays and the scientists watching me, but mostly I can feel Finn very carefully *not* watching, and the weight of the information that is now out in the open.

I've had a lot of theories about who Finn is and why he's important. Wild ones—a prince of Wales stuck here after the apocalypse began. And ones that made no sense—the illegitimate son of the president, protecting his sister.

But not this. I could never imagine this.

"Why are you here, O'Malley?" Levine asks.

"My partner came through here. With one of your Priests. I'd like to find them."

One of the Grays frowns. "A Black priest came through two days ago. But he was alone and only stayed for a few hours."

Finn's face tightens. "Is that normal? For a Black to travel alone and that quickly? Aren't they usually sent out in squadrons?"

The Grays shift and exchange looks. I laugh. "Yes. But they don't want to admit it. And certainly not to you."

Finn's gaze flashes to me, furious and warning, but I ignore him. "Finish this up, O'Malley. I've had about as much hospitality as I can take from this Haven."

I turn away. Behind me the Grays are muttering amongst themselves, and I know I did exactly what he didn't want—I drew attention, and the very worst kind at that.

I don't particularly care, even if I should.

"What do you know about Synthrix mutations?"

Finn hesitates. Of course he does. How many times has he told the Havens, and how many have ignored him? We've seen the changes in the Horde. The change is impossible to ignore—the infects are developing a pack mentality. They've always moved in groups, but they were drawn by hunger. They weren't driven by each other.

But now? Now, it seems like they are. I think back to the Horde in the Clean house, the way they moved together, almost aware of each other.

We've been fighting a war for twenty years, a war we're slowly losing. But something about it has changed—something about *them*. And now the Order is offering to listen to Finn. How the hell do I expect him to resist? I glance back at him, find him staring at me. Expression completely inscrutable. Mine isn't. Mine says so much. How angry I am, how betrayed. How much I don't want to be here. That he is breaking his promise by staying when we should find Collin. I let him see it all, and see his face tighten. A little.

Then I turn away and walk out of the lab.

I lose track of time as I sit outside the lab. Medics come and go, leveling curious looks at me, but my mind is spinning and I ignore them, content to ride the emotions and confusion. Occasionally, I hear loud voices from the lab, but they aren't clear enough for me to make sense of them.

It doesn't matter. None of it does. The only thing that really matters right now is how I'm going to deal with this new knowledge.

Sylvia Cragen. What the ever-loving fuck?

Emilie Milan was the child who began the apocalypse, the little girl who was so terrifying as a child that her parents medicated her for a lifetime, calling it a success when she went on to live a happy life.

But there was a child before her. If Emilie was the beginning of the story, he was the prologue.

Everyone has heard whispers about the violent brother who spurred Sylvia to find a way to live. I wonder vaguely if I will be given the truth now. Knowing what I do about Finn, I doubt it.

Chapter 29. A Story of Family

Finn closes the door of our room with careful precision. I pace the room, noting the clean bed and the soft carpet under my feet. It's an immaculate room, one that is reserved for visiting dignitaries.

It's more than a little surprising that they care that much about Finn. Or maybe it's a healthy fear.

"Is she still alive?" I ask abruptly.

Finn releases the breath he's been holding and drops his bag onto the bed. "We don't have to do this, Nurrin."

"I think we do, O'Malley. Or is it Cragen?" I shoot back. "What the hell have you told me that is true? Is *any* of it true?"

His eyes flash, furious. "I have never fucking lied to you, Nurrin. Be careful with those accusations."

"I want the fucking truth. No dissembling, no dodging. Tell me the truth for once."

Finn stares at me for a long moment. I wait, half holding my breath. Will he?

"Don't think you've earned something from me just because I got you off," he says, looking away.

I stare at him, not entirely sure I believe I heard him right. Then I laugh, a shrill noise. "Fuck you, O'Malley. I didn't earn anything for kissing you, except a hot shower to get the dirt off." His gaze darts to mine and goes icy. "I deserve to know this because I've fought with you. I've listened to you. I've trusted you to keep me alive, you arrogant asshole. The very least you could do is mention that your fucking mother is the creator of this goddamn plague!"

There is a long moment of silence, and then I snort. So fucking typical.

“She didn’t mean for this to happen,” he says, his voice very tired. “All she wanted was—” He cuts off, shaking his head. I want to push for more, but he moves away from me, shuffling through his bag onto the bed before he heads for the door. “We won’t be here long. I’m meeting with the Grays tonight to finish our discussion. I want you to stay here.”

“Finn,” I say, my voice low.

He looks back at me when he reaches the door. “What did I promise? Do you remember?”

I’ll keep you alive. I’ll keep Collin alive.

I nod, unhappily, and Finn studies me, looking for god knows what. Then he turns and leaves me alone. With only my thoughts and questions for company.

I’m half asleep when he comes back. I blink sleepily into the pillow, but I don’t move to look at him.

His gait is awkward—not the smooth strides of a predator, but stumbling and half falling. He lands on the bed, and I can smell the shine on him, even from here. My nose wrinkles in distaste, and I burrow deeper into my pillow. Finn is still and silent for so long I think he's passed out, and then he shifts to strip noisily out of his weapons belt and shirt. I heart the rasp of his zipper, and then he falls into bed with me. I lie there silently, and am drifting to sleep when he says, softly, "She was trying to fix him. That's all she wanted. That's all any of us wanted."

What was it like, I wonder, to grow up with Sylvia Cragen for a mother and Keifer as your uncle?

His arm comes around me, drawing me into him. I force myself to stay limp and relaxed. He thinks I'm sleeping—he has to. He would never speak to me like this, so unguarded. It feels like a lie to let him. But I'm not going to stop him. He tucks me into his side, a warm hand heavy on my hip.

"Why can't you trust me?" he mumbles.

I don't answer, and he says nothing else. But it is a very long time before I fall asleep.

Chapter 30. Atonement

I wake up sprawled across Finn, his breath in my hair, my hand in his shirt. For a moment, I don't move, not quite able to process the warm, hard body under mine, and then common sense kicks me in the ass and I start to scramble away.

His arms tighten, snagging me back against him. "Where are you going?"

"My side of the bed," I say dryly. He doesn't release me, and I put up a little fight. Amusement flares in his eyes, and his arms tighten, just enough to let me know he could keep me there. And then he lets go and I scramble across the bed to my corner. I stare at him as he stretches lazily and rolls off the bed.

A tiny treacherous part of me wants to drag him back in.

Finn throws a knowing smirk over his shoulder, and I flush, looking away.

"How long will we be here?" I ask, falling backward onto my pillow. It smells faintly of alcohol and Finn, and I want to mind more than I do.

"I want to leave today. It'll depend on what happens with the Panel."

"We have to find Collin," I remind him.

Impatience flares on his face. "I haven't forgotten. But warning the Havens was his idea—and we will never have a better audience than this one."

"You have a debt to pay, O'Malley—or you think you do. I get that. But the only thing I need is to find my brother. I'm leaving to do that—tomorrow morning. With or without you."

"Don't threaten me, Nurrin. I don't like it."

I smirk. "And wouldn't that be awful—for you to deal with something you don't like."

Laughter and annoyance are fighting in his eyes, but he shakes his head and turns away.

"Come on. Get dressed. I want to show you something."

I hesitate, staring at him as he pulls a pair of pants on and buckles them. Clean, faded blue jeans that fit his ass just right. A tight black t-shirt. And his weapons belt.

I swallow hard, looking away and scrambling for my leathers. "Where do you keep finding clean clothes?" I ask. "The end of the fucking world, and you'll go out looking like you just did your damn laundry."

Finn laughs, a silent noise that crinkles his eyes up just a little. "Always with the questions, Ren."

Chapter 31. The Wide, Wide World

I have lived my entire life behind walls. I've lived that way, happily, convinced it was safe, the only way to live. I have embraced it, because I've known no other way. Even with the walls, the sky arched overhead, and I knew how big the world was. I was happy there, in my tiny corner of it, with my brother and Dustin.

I was an idiot.

Seeing the ocean for the first time is exhilarating and terrifying, bringing tears to my eyes. Finn stands a few feet away, watching silently. I take a few stumbling steps toward the water then fall into it.

The ocean is like a living thing, a seething monster that stretches forever, curving to meet the horizon, thrashing with white-capped waves. It is alive and gorgeous and so much more than I could ever anticipate. It's a whole world, one wild and untouched by infection.

I taste salt on my lips, and I'm not sure if it's from the water breaking on my knees and splashing my face, or from the tears I wasn't aware I was crying.

"Why did we let them win?" I whisper the question. I don't need to speak louder than a whisper—Finn is too aware of me and my moods to miss it.

"Because we were terrified. Because living a small life was better, to some minds, than no life."

I twist to look at him. "Do you believe that?" I hold his gaze for a moment before I am looking back at the water, the wild ocean.

He moves, crouching near me. The water laps at his boots, a soft plea.

"I was born in Scotland. The highlands were my playground when I was a boy. My cousin and I would roam the hills behind Mum's lab. It was a whole world—hills and cliffs and more green than you could possibly imagine.

We lived inland, but every year, Da would get leave, and we'd go down to the shore. I loved the ocean then."

"Why did you come here?" I ask, hardly daring to believe he's being this open.

"Mum knew there would be side effects from Synthrix. Da had friends in the government, so we came to talk. We had bad timing." His lips twist in a grim smile. "Mum was at the CDC when Atlanta was overrun."

I jerk, staring at him. He won't look at me, and I can see the exhaustion and pain in his eyes, things he usually keeps hidden.

"No, Nurrin. A small life is not better. A small life, in the walls of a cage, isn't a life—it's a slow death."

I inhale sharply, tasting the salt of the ocean on my lips, the scent of things wild and untamable—untouched by even the infected.

"We have to find him, O'Malley. Whatever you think you can achieve here—we have to find Collin." I finally look away from the water, the mesmerizing waves, and look at him. "You have a promise to keep."

A smile ticks his lips, but it doesn't reach his eyes.

I look back at the water before I ask my question. "When we find him, can we come back here? To a Haven by the ocean?"

"Why?"

"Because I'd never ask Collin to live outside the walls—but here, I can almost pretend they don't exist."

He moves, fast, and I yelp as he catches me by the arm, his hand tangling in my ponytail hanging over my shoulder. His expression is fierce, furious.

"What?" I gasp.

"Don't. Don't ever pretend, Nurrin. Live in the walls, if that is the life you want. Or *live* outside them. But don't take this paltry existence and pretend it's more than it is. Don't fucking lie to yourself."

"Why does it matter to you?" I demand. Shock fills his eyes, and something—very deep—that I can't name. Then it's gone, and so is he. So suddenly I over balance and land in the water, my hands splashing down hard. I stay that way for a long minute, blinking the salt water off my eyelashes. I can feel Finn moving, leaving me.

Apparently sharing time is over.

Chapter 32. Panel Decision

"We think you could help us," Dr. Prachard says earnestly.

"And I appreciate your goals. I think you should keep working. Look at what the disease has done—try to predict what it will do next. But I can't help you. I'm not trained, and I'm needed elsewhere."

"What could possibly be more important than finding a cure?"

Finn sighs. "You can't cure ERI-Milan. It's too different from what was created in the lab—and it's in all of us. How will you cure us all?"

"What would you suggest?"

"Figure out a way to live—the Havens won't stand forever," he says. "You have to figure out a way to live outside the walls—to survive in the Wide Open."

"How?"

Finn blinks. "I have no idea. Surviving is a personal thing—you figure it out for yourself. I can't help you with that."

"You want to leave," one of the other scientists, Dr. Browning, says. None of them look surprised. Neither do the Gray Priests behind them.

"I came here searching for my partner," Finn says carefully. "That hasn't changed. He is still my first priority."

"With the changes you say are happening in the Horde, is traveling in the Wide Open safe? You can stay here, show us what we're doing wrong."

"You can atone for your mother's mistake," Browning chimes in. His eyes are hard, where his tone is full of false calm.

I can feel the change in Finn—tiny changes a stranger might not notice. A slight straightening of his back. The insolent twist to his lips. The hardening of his eyes. Whatever they thought to get from him, to achieve from this meeting—it's gone now. Finn has closed off from them.

I smile.

"My mother's only mistake was letting your government touch something she created with love. I have nothing to atone for. You can cut up as many rotting bodies as you want—do it till the day the Horde overruns the last Haven for all I care. I can't help you." He shifts his attention to the Grays, completely dismissing the Panel.

"Where did he go? The Black that was here."

"That is, I'm afraid, classified," A Gray priest says softly.

"Then I want access to the Stronghold. Your wireless network."

I hiss in a breath. Those are insanely expensive. The wealth of information that so many took for granted was merely one of the many things ripped apart by the infects. Very few had the money or means to put it back into place—it was limited to the largest Haven schools and government business.

"That's not possible."

Finn's hand dips into his pocket, and he pulls out a long, thin chain, smooth metal tags dangling from one end. He tosses it to the Gray, and I watch the glitter of the light on the dog tags, the narrowed eyes that widen as he reads them. Finn's cool smile.

"Your High Priest says it is."

The computer is ancient. A big monitor that has cracks and stains, a fat box to the side that spits ominous noises as we wait and watch.

But when the screen crackles to life and Omar appears, his shaved head gleaming from the lights of his office, the disrepair and alarming noises fade away, replaced by awe that something like this is possible.

"O'Malley. What do you need? And why are you threatening my people?" Omar scowls.

"I didn't threaten anyone. I think your people have a bit of a complex. I need information—there was a Black priest here, three days ago. Traveling alone. I need to know where he went."

The High Priest frowns, but leans back, and I hear the whisper of paper as he flips through whatever is on his desk. I hear a mutter that sounds vaguely like a curse, and then he's back, his face filling up the screen, a giant even here. I shiver and shift a little behind O'Malley.

"You won't like this. Why do you need this priest?"

"He has something I want," Finn says, predictably cryptic.

Something flickers in Omar's eyes, filling his face before it goes blank. "He reported in at 6 then left for his next destination. He's going to our base outside the walls of 1."

Part 3. The Guilt of Surviving

Guilt is useless. The dead don't feel guilt for dying—why feel guilt for living?

-Finn O'Malley

In this world, we are all survivors. It is our one great unifier, the only thing that could defeat our differences.

President Buchman, State of the Union Address

Chapter 33. Homecoming

I sit on top of the ZTNK, smoking. I can hear Nurrin below me, cursing as she rattles around inside the RV. She doesn't like that we're leaving it behind—I don't either. It's become something familiar, comfortable, too quickly.

One reason to leave it behind.

I can see 1 from here, the top of her walls shining in the sun. Crops circle the Haven like a giant fucking rainbow. It's the height of stupidity and arrogance to have the fields outside the Walls—but it's also typical of 1.

They have never believed the same rules apply to them here. And to be completely fair, they have never needed to.

When the Atlanta fell, everyone quickly realized it was only a matter of time before the infection spread out of control. Da more than most, and we were positioned to advise and help. The priority then was protecting the government. No one could imagine a world without something like a central government.

The Super Max had been Da's idea. Walls meant to keep people in would surely keep infects out. And they did. The prison became a fortress, and people convinced themselves it was a home.

Twenty years later, staring at it, nothing of the original structure remains except for a single watchtower. Kelsey and I played in that tower, when we still believed the war could be won, before we realized just how futile it all was. Before Kelsey became the Thrasher.

I shake my head and shift, wincing as my knees pop.

"You about ready, O'Malley?"

Her voice drifts like a memory, and I can hear another girl saying that, a lifetime ago. I lean over the side of the RV and smirk down at her. She's wearing black leathers, a tight tank top under her zom gear. Her hair is up in a messy pony tail, bits and pieces falling out onto her face. She huffs impatiently, displacing a few before they drift back down and land on her lips.

"Come *on*, Finn," she says impatiently.

I smirk and step off the side of the RV, crouching to absorb the blow to my knees when I hit the hard-packed ground. Nurrin's eyes are resolutely unimpressed. "Are you done?"

"Everything packed?"

She gives me a dirty look, and I arch an eyebrow. "Let's go, then."

There is no way to return to 1 without it causing waves. No way to slip in unnoticed. 1 is too fortified, and I am too well known. It's worked to my advantage in the past, but I'm not sure what kind of reception I'll get now.

Most people who knew me well enough to hate me are dead, so that's helpful.

Nurrin is a quiet twitching presence next to me as we pull up, and I slide a glance at her. "What is the only thing that matters?"

Her eyes are frowning, but she says the words. I nod and tap the gas enough to get the attention of the Walkers. Useless, since I've already got it.

I roll the window down as two Walkers approach.

"Name and Haven."

A deep breath. Everything will change if I do this. I slide a glance at her.

"Finn O'Malley, returning to Haven 1."

Chapter 34. Returning Hero

It's madness, predictably. The requisite blood tests, efficient blood sticks. The now-familiar moment of panic before Nurrin's settles as clean. The search for weapons, too solicitous.

And then we're being rushed through the Haven streets, and I can hear the Walkers muttering around us, my name and Kelsey's.

I had hoped, after years away, the stories would have died.

I knew better, but hope is the one thing that will always fuck you up. My lips twist a little. The Captain is speaking into his walkie, and I lean forward, away from the wide-eyed Nurrin. "I don't want to be announced."

"Sorry, sir," he says apologetically. "Orders."

I bite down on the question. Who the fuck is giving orders regarding me? Everyone is dead. My father, the war generals, Kelsey's elite team. Even the president who held this country together when the end of the world fractured it. They're all dead, and I'm left here, wondering every day what the fuck I'm doing.

It would be easier to stop. To take my weapon and chances in the Wide Open.

I would have—I meant to. Nurrin leans forward, her chin almost on my shoulder. I shift away from her, irrationally annoyed.

Where would I be, what would have happened if I hadn't stumbled into her in 8, spitting mad and cursing at a Walker who was dragging her away from the Wall?

Probably dead, and wouldn't that be nice.

"It's so big," she whispers. Her eyes are saucers on her face, reflecting the wonder of this Haven.

I remember cities, before. Sprawling things with massive shopping centers, wide roadways, trucks that sold food, and restaurants you could drive up to and have food handed out. There was very little structure, no curfew, no rules. There were parks with equipment just for children to crawl on and areas just for the dogs to run.

It was nothing like the average Haven.

The only place that comes close to the freedom that cities achieved is here, with wide spaces for parks, large trading halls, a cafeteria that serves food to everyone, not just Walkers. Even this—even here—does not approach what a city was. But to a girl from 8, who has never seen anything beyond her own walls, it's a whole different world.

I feel a surge of pride that she will see this with me, that I will protect and guide her through this. And a bolt of fear that I will lose her to this.

Not mine.

I have to continue to remind myself of that—that as much as I want her, as much as I will protect her, she isn't mine.

Nurrin values trust. And she has reluctantly given me hers. But there is so much I haven't told her—things I refuse to tell her.

The truck comes to a gentle halt, and I look around. My stomach drops. "Why are we here?" I demand, furious.

"Orders," the Captain says nervously. I swallow my snarl of outrage and turn to Nurrin.

"Stay in the car."

Her eyebrows go up, silent disbelief.

"If you have ever trusted me—do it now. Stay in the car, Nurrin. Please."

I see indecision flicker in her eyes, and then she nods and sits back. It's not a lot, and I know how quickly it can change—how quickly she will change her mind and bolt after me. Which means I need to move.

I'm out of the truck and striding up to the small white house without waiting for the Walker escort, without needing any direction. I know this place, possibly better than some of the raw recruits they've brought up since I left.

It's the same. A lot of things here have changed—a lot of things will continue to change in 1—but one thing won't. One thing will always be the same. And that is this little white house.

A man, a few years younger than me, comes out and gives me a wide smile. "Well, I'll be damned. I thought they were lying. Or dragging up a ghost who had an uncanny resemblance."

"That's a helluva lot of escorts for a ghost, Kenny," I say, letting my accent thicken. Something flares in his eyes, there and gone before I can assess it.

He moves quickly, fast enough that instinct has me reaching for my knife before I can stop the motion, but before I reach the empty sheath, he's there, his arms coming around me in a gruff hug. "It's good to have you home."

This isn't home. It hasn't been home for over ten years. I don't bother arguing with him though.

"What brings you back?"

"I'm looking for someone—my partner from Walking in 8. He was traveling with a Black Priest, and I have it on good authority that they headed this way."

Kenny smirks. "You've never been a fan of the Order, Finn."

"Still not. Omar is the Black High Priest. He owes me a favor."

I see the rage, clearly this time. Kenny has gotten good at hiding his emotions, but he can't hide that.

"What the hell are you doing associating with him, Finn? He killed her!"

"The dead aren't my burden, Kenny. Not anymore. My duty is to the living, and I'll use whatever I have at my disposal to see the living returned to me."

"Tilting at windmills again, friend?" he says, too softly.

I step back and study him. Kenny had never been a big feature in my life. Kelsey dominated my world—two years older and so perfect it was maddening. Kenny was her annoying brother, an afterthought, if we thought at all.

But that was before the war.

"I thought this house went to the current head of state."

Kenny shoves his hands in his pockets, gives me a cryptic smile. "It does."

The door to the car opens. I've taken too long. But this new information is too much, too much to dismiss or process. I stare at him, unbelieving.

And see the naked shock, the wild hope. He takes a step, almost staggering as she slips her hand into mine.

"Kelsey?" he whispers, his voice shaking.

Nurrin makes an impatient noise and looks at me. "We're wasting time."

I'm still staring at Kenny. I see hope fade, replaced by devastation and the realization that, as much as she looks like Kelsey—and with her hair up and her leathers wrapped around her like skin, she does—it's not her, just a lovely stand-in. She is a ghost, haunting this home.

Hunger flickers in his eyes, and then it's gone, locked away as he licks his lips and forces a smooth smile. "We haven't met."

And if there was any way to avoid this meeting, I would—I think I would rather face a horde than do this. But Kenny is looking at me, his eyes demanding, and Nurrin is twitching impatiently.

"Nurrin, Kendall Buchman."

She smiles, a pretty dimple appearing in one cheek, and I'm reminded of how innocent she still is, despite her time with me and the sharp edges I seem to hone.

"Buchman, huh? Any relation to the late president?"

"He was my father," Kenny says smoothly. He's still holding her hand, even though the handshake is over. I can't help staring at it, and Nurrin flushes, pulling her hand free.

"I'm sorry," she murmurs, a soft acknowledgment of everyone Kenny has lost.

When your father is the president, your loss is a public tragedy, but it's no more than the private ones we have all faced since the world ended.

Nurrin refocuses on me. "Does he have any information on Collin?"

I grit my teeth. "I was in the process of finding that out, when you decided to join us. What happened to the damn car?"

Her expression goes sticky sweet. "Got hot."

I don't imagine the snort of laughter from Buchman, but I do manage, barely, to ignore it.

"I'll send word to the Order's Priestess. If your Black Priest is here, we'll find him. In the meantime, my Walkers will see you settled at the hotel."

Nurrin blinks. "You have a hotel?"

Kenny grins, the same charming smile his father used to win reelection. Except it looks different on him—menacing in a way Andrew never was. Or maybe it's because the smile is aimed at Nurrin, and I can feel the way she sways toward him. "We need somewhere for Aldermen to stay when they come into town. I've already called and had two rooms prepared for you."

Nurrin tenses next to me then grins happily.

Mother fucking happily.

I know she hates me. I know we're only together because she has no options, not if she wants to find Collin. But that she is so happy to be away from me—I shake the thought, refuse to dwell on it, and say, smoothly, "No need. I still have my house here."

Something crosses his face, and I go very still. Rage flickers in my veins. He didn't—.

"That place was mine. Deeded to me for my service under the Thrasher and in the war."

"Her name," Kenny growls furiously, "was Kelsey." The easy-going smile is gone, and the man who stands here is capable of running our nation, even fractured as it is. It is the first time in my life I've felt a smidge of respect for him.

Except his anger sparks my own. "I know her name, Kenny. I spent years with her—don't forget that."

"As if my father would have let me," he spits.

"Is that what this is about?" I ask, letting a little contempt slip into my voice. It might be the equivalent of poking a bear, but his self-righteous bullshit is grating on nerves—already raw from being somewhere I don't want to be.

"Do we have to do this?" Nurrin cuts in sharply. "You can glare at each other later—I want a shower and a clean bed. Who can make that happen?" She looks at me expectantly.

"What happened to my house?" I grit out the question.

"Stay at the Embassy tonight. I'll see about your house, and you can move back in tomorrow."

I don't like it. But I know she's tired, and I don't want to fuck with Kenny today—I want to use the rest of the day to reach out to the friends I still have in 1. So I nod. Success gleams briefly in his eyes. "Excellent. Let's go."

He draws alongside Nurrin, and I stalk behind them, silently seething. At first she is startled, but that gives way quickly to amusement as Kenny rattles off places in 1 that she should visit and asks innocuous questions about where we've been, what we've been doing, who we are looking for.

It annoys the ever-loving fuck out of me. Not because she tells him anything—she's a First, a survivor, and too fucking smart for that shit—but because I can tell the attention is alluring. And I don't want her fucking allured.

I throw myself into the front seat, kicking the Captain out as Kenny helps Nurrin into the backseat, and remind myself that I have no right to be jealous. She isn't mine.

She never will be.

If I could just fucking remember that, life would be much easier for all of us.

Chapter 35. The Embassy

Kenny walks us in. By now, he's found reasons to reach out and touch her. She's got a tiny smile on her lips that makes me want to throttle the both of them. That fucking fast. Logic tells me to back off—Kenny isn't a bad guy, just one I dislike.

I dislike a lot of people.

He steps over to the desk, and I lean into her space. "Forget that kiss already, little girl?"

She twists, a wisp of hair falling into her eyes as she smirks at me. "Jealous?"

Yes. She pauses, her head tilting slightly as she stares, fascinated. What can she see in my eyes?

"O'Malley," Kenny calls. I pull away from Nurrin, cursing softly even as I stare at her. She is such a bad idea. If I could just remember that. "Is a queen ok?"

"Give us the suite," I say abruptly, not looking away from Nurrin. Her eyes go wide, and anger colors her cheeks.

Now I look away, right into Kenny's angry blue eyes, just before he grins and nods. He's gotten good at hiding what he's feeling. I suppose nine years and a presidency will do that.

"What happened to age restrictions for your office?" I ask lazily.

Even the unflappable receptionist reacts to that question, a shocked little gasp. Kenny smiles slightly. "Does it bother you?"

"It doesn't affect me. I don't give a fuck about shit that doesn't affect me."

The receptionist mouth forms a startled little *O*, and Nurrin vibrates with anger at my side.

Kenny just stares at me.

I step up to the desk and give the receptionist a cool smile. "Keys?"

"Suite 102. On the tenth floor, sir," she says faintly. I think her professional curtsy is more habit anything at this point. I take Nurrin's arm and pull her into me. "Thanks, Kenny. Appreciate the escort."

I turn away and get halfway across the lobby before his voice rings out behind me. "It's Kendall, O'Malley. Or better yet—President Stiles."

I don't look back.

Chapter 36. In The Suite

She shakes my arm off as soon as we're in the elevator. I eye the contraption briefly then shake my head, annoyed. Only fucking 1 would have something as ridiculously frivolous as an elevator. Damn politicians and their fucking obsession with keeping the world the same. It's not. It can't be. The rest of the world has adjusted—when are they going to wake the fuck up?

"What was that?" she asks softly. She's not as angry as I expect, and that throws me off.

"Kenny Buchman Stiles. We"—I make a face—"grew up together. Sort of."

"You hate him."

I blink at her, startled. Nurrin laughs. "Come on, O'Malley. You all but peed on me to mark your territory. You embarrassed him in front of his people. You challenged him." She smirks. "You weren't this aggressive with Omar."

"I can kill Omar," I say reasonably.

It should bother me more, that I can say that *reasonably.*

"Can't assassinate the president of the United States, can you?" she muses. "Why do you hate him, O'Malley?"

"Mind your own fucking business, Nurrin. I'm going to shower and head out."

She trails me into the bathroom, "Where are you going?"

I stop stripping to stare at her. "What does it matter? I'm not taking you. You aren't leaving this fucking room, do you hear me? I don't trust this haven, or Kenny. He'll have people watching us."

"Paranoid much?" she asks.

"My paranoia keeps me alive. And you, as well. Remember that."

She rolls her eyes, and I nudge her toward the door. I need a moment, a space of breath between us.

“Why did you do it?” she asks, tilting her head back to look at me.

I don’t ask her what she’s talking about. I sigh and lean against the sink. I need sleep, so fucking bad. It feels like I haven’t slept since 8 fell.

“Do you really want to do this, Nurrin? Because we’ve done pretty good, ignoring it.”

“Can’t ignore the elephant forever,” she shoots back. I bite down on my tongue to keep from saying something snarky to her. Glance at her from under my eye lashes.

“Biological needs, Nurrin. You were there. I was there. It was fun. Nothing more.”

Her eyes go wide and startled, and then she nods, too abruptly. “Nothing more. Good. Then you’ll excuse me if I don’t want you marking me as yours. Kendall wants to have dinner with me.”

I raise an eyebrow. “When did that happen?”

"On the way here. Weren't you listening?"

"I don't want you spending time with him, Nurrin. He's dangerous."

"Says the man who would happily kill the Black Priest," she says mockingly as she pushes away from the wall. "Keep your hands off me, Finn. We're traveling together. Nothing more."

"Not even you could make yourself believe that, Nurrin," I say softly.

She gives me a thin-lipped smile. "I'm very adept at believing the truth."

The door to her room is closed when I emerge from the shower. I consider knocking on it, but she doesn't want to talk to me—she's made that very clear. A closed door speaks volumes.

So I dress quickly, grab a few knives and my gun belt. Shove my feet into some dusty boots. "Stay here," I shout.

"Fuck you, O'Malley," she shouts back, amiably.

I grin and head out.

When I left 1, I swore I'd never come back. With Da dead, Buchman dying, and Kelsey worse than dead, I had nothing to keep me here but bad memories. There was a lot of anger over that last mission, and not many were sad to see me go.

There were a few, though. And those few are who I go to now.

Claire Donal was in the US visiting her new niece when the dead rose. She was one of the ex-pats Da scrapped together and evacuated to 1. A lot of them didn't survive. They didn't know how to survive in this new world, one so separated from the one that they always known. Claire, on the other hand, did. She didn't just survive in 1, she thrived.

In Ireland, she had been a town gossip, a skill that proved useful in our new world. She knew everything that was happening in the city and had no problems bartering that knowledge for anything she needed.

If there was anything I missed about 1, it was her.

Claire didn't like the pretense most of 1 embraced—she didn't have a shop in the market district, to peddle her information.

She's a creature of comfort—she likes to be at home with her hot tea in front of her and her feet buried under a rug. If you have information, you can damn well come to her.

Which is what I am doing now. The house is quiet—no one's around it, but that could be because of the hour of the day. I tap on the door, and when I hear her voice, push it open. Her eyes go very wide when she sees me, and she makes a little noise like a shriek. I smirk, and she screams at me.

"What the hell are you doing here?" she demands.

"It seemed like a good time to come home."

"This isn't your home. It hasn't been since—" She stops abruptly, and her face takes on a slightly apologetic look. Her eyes find mine. I shake my head.

"Don't worry about it. It was a long time ago."

"It was. But not so long ago that you've forgotten."

I shrug. "It's hard to forget something you live through."

"Especially when you shouldn't have?" she asks archly.

My expression goes a little cold, and she laughs. "Don't bother with that—it's never worked on me. I saw you grow up, remember?"

"Bitch," I say, fondly.

"What are you doing here?" she asks. "I thought the world would end before O'Malley came home to 1."

"Didn't that happen twenty years ago?"

She gives me a look that's hard to read, even for me, then stands. "I'm going to make us some tea, and then you're going to tell me what the hell you're doing here."

She's still bossy as fuck.

Some things really will never change, I think, following her to the kitchen and watching as she putters around boiling tea and dropping in old tea bags.

Part of me wants to ask where she's still getting her supply of tea, but I don't—some things about Claire you just leave alone and let be a mystery. We all deserve a few secrets.

She hands me a cup of bitter brew, and we go back to the living room. I wait as she settles into her chair. "Not that I'm not thrilled to see you—of course, I am. But what the fuck are you doing here, O'Malley?"

I hesitate, not sure what to tell her. And then I say, "There's a girl."

Claire laughs. "There always is, with you. Is it like Kelsey?"

Again, I hesitate, weighing the question. So many ways to answer. Because in ways—yes. They could pass as sisters, she is so similar to Kelsey. But there are differences, a refreshing innocence about Nurrin that Kelsey never had—couldn't have, in the world we knew.

"Of a sort," I say finally.

"I've heard bits and pieces about you over the years, O'Malley. You haven't made many friends in the West."

"Did you think I would?" I ask.

Claire's eyes soften, a little. "I had hoped, darling boy."

I don't respond—Claire has always been good at seeing through and calling me on my bullshit. And has absolutely no qualms in loving me, despite my faults.

"What is happening in the Haven?" I ask softly. "How the hell did Kenny win the presidency? Have they lost all sense?"

"He ran on the family ticket. Even using his mother's maiden name, he was something familiar. With everything that's happening, familiar is nice. It was necessary." She shrugs. "And frankly, he hasn't been a bad president. The Havens have done well under him."

I snort, "The ones that survive. The ones the infects haven't taken."

Her eyes narrow on me, and she takes a deliberate sip of her tea before setting it aside. "What the hell are you talking about?"

I get up, pacing anxiously. "Same currency?"

Claire has the grace to look offended. "You don't buy information, O'Malley. You're a friend. I won't demand payment from you."

"And I won't take your charity," I say gently. Something flickers in her eyes, grateful respect.

"The Havens are falling," I say bluntly. "Seven in the past year. That we know about. The zombies are changing—ERI-Milan has always been a disease of mutation, and I think it's had another jump. I think our time behind these walls—in the safety of the Havens and the Walkers—it's coming to an end."

"The Havens have been safe for twenty years, O'Malley. You can't waltz in here and say that's going away. People won't believe you."

"I don't care what people believe. They can accept the truth, or they can ignore it—neither makes it less true." I pace the length of the room. "You can't stay here—they *will* come to 1. The hordes will keep moving until there is nothing. The infection doesn't burn off—we won't cure it."

"And you came to 1 to deliver this message? Seems incredibly altruistic for you, O'Malley."

"My partner," I say softly. "He's missing. I think he came here with a Black priest. It's the only reason I'm back."

She studies me for a moment. Then, "Stiles will insist on making this a state visit. You know that, right?"

I give Claire a tight little smile, my eyes going cold. "Kenny can go fuck himself."

"That won't be a popular opinion here, darling. The boy has done well by us. And people still remember you and your loyalty to the First Family."

"It wasn't to the family, Claire. You know that. It was to *her,*" I say.

"So what will you do? Alienate the man who can help you?"

I don't answer, because I don't know what to say. Accepting Kenny's help goes against my best instincts—and my instincts have served me well to keep me alive.

“I’ll put up with it, to a point. I need time to get everything together in 1 and to find Collin.”

“What are you going to do?” she asks.

“I haven’t decided yet, but you are right about one thing. This isn’t home anymore. I’m done here. This will be my last time in 1.” Sorrow fills her eyes, and I lean in to give her a kiss on the cheek. "Thank you for everything. I would have been lost here without you."

"Of course. Do you want me to come if there's a party? You might need a few people who like you."

I think about Ren, with all of her questions unanswered, and this woman who knows too much about me. "No. I think it would be best if I didn't have allies."

A smile turns her lips. “You can't protect her or hide her forever."

"Probably not, but I'll give it a damn good shot."

Claire laughs, a solid, hearty noise that follows me as I leave her house.

Chapter 37. State Parties

I will say this about Kenny: he moves damn fast.

The room is a mess of dresses and glittering shoes when I return. Nurrin is grinning like an idiot and talking to an effeminate man in his mid forties.

I don't say anything, just stop and stare with my eyebrows raised. She smirks. “Kendall is throwing you a party to welcome you home formally.”

“Well,” I say, “that's very nice of him. Glad he asked me if I could clear my schedule first.”

She snorts and turns away from me to discuss dress choices with the other man, effectively dismissing me from the entire conversation.

Little Nurrin has grown balls in the time we’ve spent together. I'm not sure what Collin will think of her when we find him.

"You should get dressed," she says over her shoulder "The party starts in an hour."

I'm tempted to argue with her and stay in what I'm wearing. I have no need to impress the officials and pompous assholes who populate this Haven. But I heave a sigh and go to my room to change.

One thing I learned quickly after the Turn: politicians don't change. Doesn't matter if the dead rose and are outside the door eating the guests, politicians stay the same—the same self-serving, power-hungry bastards who have nothing else in life to do but spend the people's money. This party promises to be more of the exact same behavior.

But it's a good excuse for Nurrin to get dressed up, and I won't pass up that opportunity. She looks fucking hot in a dress. She's picked a jade green one tonight, with a low back and high Mandarin collar that wraps around her smooth throat. It contrasts sharply with her blonde hair and green eyes, and I want her, a sharp pang of desire that hits like they always do—unexpectedly and with the force of a bullet.

She gives me a slow look, taking in my suit, the jacket hanging open, and slicked back hair.

"How many weapons are you carrying?" I ask, stepping into the living room.

Her eyes sparkle with sad amusement—it's the same question her brother asks, every morning.

"Three."

I almost ask about ammo, but I don't. The fact that she's managed to hide three weapons—at least one gun—in that sexy as sin dress is too much of a turn on.

"You know this is going to be a mad house, don't you?" I say softly. She's turned away from me, the smooth expanse of her back a wide oval of unmarked skin. I itch to trace the curve of her spine, trail kisses down to where her back flares to meet her ass. Push her until she's panting and begging.

"It'll be fun. Kendall promised to show me around the Haven after."

I go still, the desire gone abruptly. "Excuse me?"

"After the party. He knew you'd probably want to see some of your old friends, so he offered to show me around a little bit. Why?"

"Nurrin," I say, practically snarl. "He's dangerous. For the love of god, stay away from him."

"You don't like him."

"I don't trust him," I correct. Her hands are in her hair, attempting to pin it up. I pluck the little pins from her fingers, let it fall, and lean past her to pick up a small decorative comb. I recognize it—of course I do.

Kenny is a sick fuck.

I tuck the comb in one side, pulling her hair out of her eyes. Nurrin lets out a shaky breath and twists to stare at me. Too close. Too much. I want too much, and I can't. Her eyes go soft and sleepy, a hint of a smile to her lips.

And I step away, giving us both the space I need to get my head on straight. Because this can't happen—not here, not now. Maybe—probably—not ever.

"Do you trust me?" I ask quietly. Because I want that. I want that so much—no one but Collin has trusted me in so long I've begun to forget what it actually feels like to not be looked at with scorn and hate.

Oh, some people, the smart ones like Lissel, will keep some respect in their eyes. But it's not for me. It's for Thrasher's solider, the one who still has ties and a past.

I hate her, for dying. For leaving me behind with this mess while she escaped. I hate myself, more, for living.

"You don't make trusting you easy," she says.

I incline my head, acknowledging that. I don't. I never will. It is who I am.

"Yes," she says.

A little bit of the tension inside me eases, and I put a shawl around her shoulders. "Come on, Ren. We're gonna be late."

The party is, quite predictably, ridiculous.

Women in slinky dresses, men in suits, not a single one of them carrying weapons.

Cater waiters—fucking cater waiters—wandering around with trays of delicacies and dishes nobody's ever heard of.

Except here. Here the stupid extravaganza is commonplace. It's nothing—just a little party to welcome home a hero.

Not that anyone believes that. No one here thinks I'm a hero. No one has for a very long time, and I can see it in the looks that they give me when I think I'm not looking.

Fuck it. And fuck them. I don't care. I watch Ren, concentrating on her as she navigates this glittering ball of vipers.

She moves through the crowd like she was born to it, with smiles and little laughs and the occasional small talk when someone stops her. Kenny is escorting her around, and that brings people's attention to her. That, and she looks just like Kelsey.

I shake my head. There is a general approaching me. I recognize him vaguely. He must have fought in the war.

For a while I'm caught up in the crowd, making small talk about the last Haven we were in, avoiding dirty looks, and hating every fucking minute of it. How on earth did I let myself get dragged here?

I manage to slip in a few questions about the Black Priest, but no one knows anything, and if they do, they aren't talking. Not surprising. The Order doesn't have much of a presence in 1—or at least they didn't when I left.

Politicians have very little use for a cult other than their own.

Somehow I manage to keep track of her, so I see when she loses it, when her eyes get a little bit too wide and her breathing little bit too fast, the smile on her face a little too stiff.

Buchman is still talking to an advisor.

Two politicians' wives are praising her dress and touching her, and I can see that she's about the bolt or snap and pull her weapon. That would make my night, but I sigh and step into action. I'm moving across the dance floor before I can stop myself.

"Nurrin," I say sharply.

She jerks, startled, and then a small smile of relief forms on her lips, quickly gone. I offer my arm, and she steps away from the other women, away from Kenny, who is approaching her, pushing into my space.

He frowns. And even though I know he's the president of the fucking United States, I have a very hard time seeing him as anything more than the little boy who followed me and Kelsey around.

“You aren't leaving are you?” he asks.

“No,” she says quickly. “I just need some air, and Finn needs my..."

"I need to talk to her,” I add, wrapping an arm around her waist.

Knowing this is rude, knowing that people are watching, I turn away without waiting for response and lead her out of the room.

The farther we get the crowd, the more she relaxes until finally she shakes my arm and says, “You have to quit doing that.”

I don't say anything, just smirk. I lead her to the back of the building to the small staircase that leads the roof.

Her eyebrows go up when she sees it. “How did you know about this?” she asks.

“Always. *Always* with the questions.”

She grins. “You would have no idea what to do with me if I quit asking questions.”

I let my eyes do a slow crawl over her, tracing from her hair, still in its comb, to the high collar of her dress, all the way down, tracing every curve along the way. Then I flick my gaze back to hers and give her a slow smile. “I could figure something out.”

She flushes. There's an interesting bit of color crawling up her neck, just enough to get me interested in how far down it goes. “Promise?” she whispers.

“Don't,” I say soft and, low my voice a warning. “Don't do this if you're not incredibly sure it's what you want.”

She steps to me, and her lips cover mine. All thoughts ceases for a few seconds. Her soft lips part, her tongue darting out to flirt with mine. I'm against her, and it takes a huge effort of will to step away. More than I thought possible, but somehow I manage it.

"Stop," I whisper. "This isn't what you want. And I don't want his sloppy seconds."

The color in her cheeks now isn't arousal—it's anger. She steps back. Frowns. "You really are an asshole, you know. I have no idea how Collin put up with you for so long."

I keep my face blank. "I'm an acquired taste, sweetheart."

She snorts. Steps away from me to peer over the Haven. The lights are on in full force tonight, illuminating the Haven, the limos that wait in the street for their respectable occupants.

How many whores will find their way into the back of those cars tonight?

"It's insane, you know?" she says softly. "I never dreamed a place like this could still exist. Collin would talk about them. Places like this. But—I just...it never seemed real. It doesn't seem real now. How do you leave a place like this?"

It's easy.

I don't like everyone knowing everything about me.

"I don't like being questioned every time I open my front door. I don't like everyone thinking they know what is right for me and being in my business. Right now, sitting there, you see it. It's beautiful and glitter and Kenny is charming. What we don't see is how fascinated they are with gossip and how much they don't care what happens outside their walls. They're selfish and self-absorbed and bored."

She's quiet, staring off into space. Softly, she says,"Havens are falling. The infection is changing. People are dying by the thousands, and 1? They don't care. They throw parties."

"I saw that a long time ago, after the war ended. I left and I found a place where I could live. It was a good place, though you hated it," I say. She's staring at me like she's never heard me speak—and to be fair, I don't usually talk *this* much.

"Collin did. Hate 8. But he would love this."

"Yeah, it's beautiful. I hope you enjoy it while we're here. Just don't forget *why* we're here. Don't let Kenny charm you out of remembering your brother."

She inhales sharply, a stinging little noise, but I don't take it back. I don't explain myself. I just leave it there. I leave the party behind—if she wants Kenny, let him bring her home

I'm downstairs, and almost to the door, when he stops me. I don't know why I didn't expect it. Or maybe I'd just deluded myself into thinking this wouldn't happen. That Kenny would be smart enough to leave me alone. But he isn't. Not terribly surprising, in retrospect.

"Nurrin—she's a lovely girl," he says, sipping at a drink. I eye him briefly. "She reminds me of Kelsey."

"That you can say that with a straight face is a little disturbing, Kenny. Kelsey was your sister, after all."

"I know exactly what she was. And I know that you are responsible for her death." His genial smile is gone, replaced with a cold mask. There it is. The man behind the charm. "I want Nurrin. And I want you out of my Haven."

"Pity I don't much give a fuck what you want," I say lazily. "I'm here looking for information. By your own family's decrees, I'm given safe passage and shelter in this Haven. You broke your own laws by violating the sanctity of my house."

"It was Kelsey's," he growls.

"And she's dead. So what the fuck do you think it matters? She deeded it to me, and I was using it, in good faith that it would be undisturbed when I returned home. You broke that faith. Not me."

"We gave her to you, in good faith that you would bring her home."

I look away, too tired for this fight. "I did," I say softly.

"You brought home a *corpse,*" he snarls. I blink. I don't want to do this. I want my quiet haven—and Collin, with no questions. I want the orchards around me as I listen to Nurrin and her friends. I want the warm sun and my bike, and I want—more than anything—I want it all to be over. This whole fucking thing.

I've been wrapped up in it—the disease, and Kelsey, and the war—for too long to ever truly separate myself from it. I should know better. I do know better.

"Are you throwing me out?" I ask softly. "And before you answer, know this—Nurrin will come with me. I won't fight for her—she'll *come* because I am still the only person who can help her find her brother. One night of charm and drinks won't distract her from that."

"Maybe not. But you are fighting an uphill battle. The Order doesn't like you—and the word about your history with Omar is filtering out of Vegas. The generals don't like you, and I can't blame them at all for that. And I don't like you. Who the hell do you think is going to take your side—stand by you—in 1?"

I cock my head and give him a smile. "What makes you think I need an ally? I've always worked very well on my own—it's one thing the Thrasher valued most about me."

I use her title on purpose—I know it annoys him. A vein pops in his forehead, and I smirk and step away from the wall. I can see Nurrin reentering the room, see the way the crowd reorients itself around her. They react to her the way I remember people around Kelsey—like she is special, something different that needs protection.

In a way, they're right. She is special. She is different, and that deserves to be treasured.

In a way, they're better for her than I am. I am too fascinated in how breaking her can make her stronger to consider protecting her. I know that she's different—but I know that as lovely and strong as she could be, there is so much more to her. There is a world of strength waiting to be discovered in her moments of weakness.

They don't see that. Dustin didn't—none of the Walkers in 8 saw it. They saw a pretty girl, another Haven girl perfect for raising the next generation and taking care of her husband—worrying about him. They didn't see a girl whose strength matched their own.

Surprise flickers on her face, and I wonder how many of my thoughts she read in my expression. I force it blank, slipping behind the mask. She frowns, but an Alderman is talking to her and she is distracted briefly. I exchange a long look with Kenny. It's on the tip of my tongue to tell him to stay away from her, but I remember the boy he was.

The more interest I show, the more he will want something just to take it from me. It's the reason he's always been fascinated with Kelsey.

"I'll send some men to escort you around the Haven tomorrow," he says, his tone firmly back in warm politician mode.

I shrug. "Don't bother. I'll be out most of the day."

He's still forming a response when I turn away. I see a party of five arriving, Priests of the Order in pristine robes. Black, Red, Gray, White, and Blue.

There is a stronger presence here than I believed. My gut twists, and I catch her eye again. They're a bit wide and a little glazed—to anyone else, she looks calm and collected. But I can see the subtle tells of fear. I arch an eyebrow and watch as she takes a deep breath, steadying herself and her nerves. She gives me a tiny nod.

And against all good sense, I leave her there, surrounded by my enemies.

Chapter 38. In Haven 1

I leave in the morning, while she is still sleeping. It was a shitty night all around—I was restless all evening, waiting for her to return, and the tension didn't die down when she did. If anything, knowing she was on the other side of the suite made it even worse. I wanted to slip into her room, into her bed, kiss her until she forgot Kenny and the politicians, her own name, forgot everything but me.

I didn't. Of course I didn't. But the temptation was there, and it was damn hard to ignore.

And sleeping was difficult—too much silence. I shared space with her for long enough that being on my own feels strange.

Which is fucked up. And fucking annoying.

I make a face and grab some fruit off a platter provided by the Embassy. Then I head out, deliberately leaving her behind.

Here's the thing. When you leave a place, it kind of freezes in your mind. Even knowing that our world is defined by blood and adaptability, it's strange to see the changes in 1. I wander the Haven for four hours, find deserted shops in the places of friends. I find my way, slowly, to the barracks.

It's where I should have started.

Being a Walker—and before that, a special forces solider—means I'm most comfortable with weapons and men who know how to use them. But even here, it's like a different world. The rooms are different, the faces filling them unfamiliar. The commander is a man I've never met, and he gives me a brief look when I'm ushered into his office. "President Stiles said you'd slip my men. I sent the best I have."

I shrug. I saw the Walkers in the Embassy lobby as I ducked out.

"Sorry," I say, completely unrepentant.

He grunts. "They've better things to do than chase a has-been war hero."

I smirk. He's got a lot disdain for a man he's never met. I wonder what Kendall told him. The Commander sits back, rubbing his eyes. Orwell is a trim man, mid-thirties, with hair that is going salt-and-pepper at the temples. His eyes are brown, and cold as they stare at me. "What the hell are you doing here, O'Malley? I've heard the stories. I know about Columbus. I've read the reports—the one President Buchman didn't have redacted. I never understood why he bothered with that. Why he protected you."

Because he trusted me. The words are on the tip of my tongue, but I don't say them. I don't say anything. I stare at him until he finally sighs. "Tell me what you want."

"A Black Priest."

Orwell's face takes on an expression of distaste, and my impression of the man inches up. "I can't help you with that. The Order is not a fan of mine."

"Why?"

He pauses, studies me. Then shrugs. "I'm new to the command—Stiles gave me the appointment a year ago. The Order had a man up for the job—one of their Black Priests. Not the High Priest. But he chose me. They haven't been happy with the president since."

"So he's not in their pocket."

"It's hard to determine. A Blue is in his cabinet, and several Grays have been made Science Czars. But for now, he's keeping the military away from the Order."

"Because of Omar. As long as he controls the Blacks, Kenny won't want anything to do with them," I say quietly. The Commander's eyebrows go up, but it makes sense.

"You don't have to have ties to the Order—but you monitor who comes into the

Haven. Have any Priests come by recently? From 6?"

"I'll have my assistant check the records. It might take a few days—we have six gates and several hundred visitors on a daily basis. You understand."

I do. But it makes me twitch with impatience. "I need this quickly. 1 is not a friendly place for me or my companion."

"Nurrin Sanders? Stiles seems very taken with her."

I nod, my lips pressed together. "That would be the issue."

Understanding and amusement fills the other man's eyes. "Don't worry. Stiles is easily distracted—another pretty face will arrive from another Haven, and he'll forget all about your girl."

For some reason, that bothers me even more.

I'm leaving the Commander's office when I see them. Kendall is dressed down, in jeans and a button down shirt with two buttons undone.

Nurrin is dressed up. She's put on a dress, of all things, and a pair of heels that stretch her legs and curve them. Her hair is up in a messy knot on the top of her head—the same way she wears it when she's fighting or working out, or when she's running the track. With the dress, it doesn't look sweaty and messy. It looks sexy, finger-tousled, and freshly fucked. She's holding his arm, her head tilted to him, a smile on her face.

I can't hear what he's saying, not from here, but I can see how incredibly beautiful she looks, and how she hangs on everything he says.

I stay in the shadows, watching as he leads her, as he settles her into a chair at a café—only in 1 would they have open air cafés. He orders for her, and I see the annoyance in her rigid shoulders before she lets it go, smiling at the waitress and Kenny.

I should leave, but I can't bring myself to move. So I lean back, into the shadows of the door way, and watch as he flirts and charms, as she asks questions and sips at the drink he selected for her. What the hell does she think she's doing? What game is she playing?

They talk for a while, until she finally shifts and stands. Kenny stands with her, and I can't see his face, but I see his move. Rage flares in me as he kisses her. But still, I watch as she leans into him, fitting against him, the soft drift of her eyelashes as she closes her eyes and brings a hand up to twist in his hair. I hiss, a soft noise I'm glad no one can hear, and then she's pulling away, a soft smile in her eyes. She says something else and moves away. I let her take three or four steps, until I know she will be sure to see me. Then I step out of the shadows clinging to the door.

Nurrin goes still, startled, her eyes wide. Her lips are still wet and lush from his kiss, color in her cheeks, but there is a touch of fear in her eyes that I know is for me. Just me.

I stare silently for a long moment, until she's fidgeting, and then I let my disgust seep through. She flinches, as if she's been struck.

Then I step past her and walk away. "Finn," she calls, once. I keep walking. There is nothing I can say to her right now that won't be violent and unforgivable.

She isn't mine. She's been with me, long enough that I've begun to forget. She can't be mine. I won't let her be.

But it doesn't mean I don't want her. And the sight of her in Kendall's arms is enough to leave me irate and shaking with violence.

Chapter 39. The Uses of the Order

The best part—the only good thing—about the Order is the vice clubs. They're a part of every Haven, and I go to one now. Anyone can fight in the ring matches. All you need is a little cash and a bit of desperation. I'm lacking on the latter, but the first is easy and I'm angry enough that I need violence to flush it from my system. Before I see her and do something neither of will be able to live with.

The Priestess who takes my money is a pretty girl in dull red robes. A blood-thirsty little bitch then. All reds are driven by blood and conversion—crazy zealots, the lot of them. She gives me an appreciative stare as I strip out of my shirt and weapons belt and hand over the money.

"You'll be fighting our Kang," she purrs. "He won a few nights back, but isn't our current champion."

I nod and push past her into the crowd. They immediately launch into the predictable chatter as they eye me. I'm not a sure bet—I don't look like the type that will beat another man into oblivion. I'm wiry instead of thick, and I don't bother playing to the crowd. I'm content to ignore them altogether and focus on the source of my real rage—her arms wrapped around Kenny, her lips wet, her hands gentle in his hair.

She was gentle with him. There'd been none of the passionate violence she gave to me, on the rare occasions I kissed her.

Each time we've kissed—the boat, the house in 18, the club, even the barracks, when I watched her fall apart under my hand—each time has been a battle, a fight for dominance that shifted into desire. There was never gentleness. Nurrin doesn't *need* gentle. She needs fire and fight, the heat of passion burning her up until there is nothing left. Until she is broken by it and so desperate for it again that putting herself together is the only option, as natural as breathing.

Kendall has no idea what she needs—what she is. He can't know, because he met her twelve fucking hours ago.

I growl, softly, as a spectator gets a little too close, and there's a nervous titter of laughter from the candy on his arm. She giggles. "He's savage. I like him."

I give her a cold smile, the last smirk from a predator before he devours his prey, and her eyes go wide and hungry.

Then the bell clangs and the far gate swings open, and Kang explodes into the ring. I watch him lazily, the arm candy forgotten as I assess my opponent. He's big—outweighs me by close to thirty pounds, with a shaved head and a fucking face tattoo. Who the fuck is this prick? Does he have no sense of what's fucking idiotic? Who the hell tattoos their face? Who the fuck kisses a man she's known for twelve. fucking. hours?

He bellows and rushes me. I slip aside, twisting around to follow him with a sharp kick to the kidneys. He reels back, and I punch him once, twice. Three times in that fucking stupid tattoo, because dammit, who the hell decided that was a good idea? He roars as he hits the mat, and I kick him again, vicious shots to the kidneys until he lies there limply and I can smell blood and shock in the air. I shake my hand out, blood spraying from it. A few of the girls shriek in mock disgust, and I bare my teeth at the crowd.

Then I retreat to my side of the ring, and money begins to change hands. I catch the Priestess' eye and nod briefly.

Once wasn't enough. It wasn't even close to enough.

I fight five more people before they pull me out of the ring. I'm snarling in rage, covered in blood, and the clear victor. The Priestess has been replaced by a Black Priest with a clinical stare. "Got a bit of anger."

"I don't see how that's any of your business," I snap. "Take your fucking cut and let me go."

"You're the victor for the evening. You'll be expected back tomorrow," he says casually.

I laugh, a mirthless noise. "Tell you what. You tell me where the Lone Priest is, and I'll come back and fight your battles tomorrow."

"We haven't had a Lone Priest in a few months," he says cautiously. I growl softly. Why is everyone hiding this man? What the hell was so special about him that even the Order is denying knowledge?

I don't say anything else, but as I take my earnings and tug my shirt on my still-bloody body, it occurs to me that reaching out to Omar again might be my only option.

Every time I do, I feel a little more indebted to him, and every time I bring them into our life, I feel the noose tighten around Nurrin's neck.

I curse and stalk back to the Embassy.

I see the wild looks the staff members give me as I stalk into their pristine lobby. The girl singing at the piano falters, swallowing a scream as I storm through the civilized room to their ridiculous elevators.

"Uh..." One of the receptionists hesitantly approaches me, and I give her a icy look.

"Don't. I know I'm offending your guests. The thing is, darling, that I don't give a fuck. You have a problem with me? Ask your president if he'll tolerate you kicking me out. I think you might be surprised by his answer."

She swallows hard, and the elevator doors glide open. The couple inside goes pale when they see me then scurry out.

I step inside and fix the receptionist with a final cool stare. "You can station a guard outside my room—but I'm not bitten, and I won't change."

My temper is still riding the edge, and that's not good—that's not how I need to confront Nurrin.

I don't *need* to confront Nurrin. I need to walk the fuck away and let some other idiot help her find her brother.

Guilt hits me immediately, and I shake my head. I can't leave Collin—or Nurrin. I swore after Columbus I would never leave anyone behind again.

I also swore I'd never give a fuck about anyone, and that was an epic fail.

I curse softly and push open the door to our suite.

Kendall has a hand on her knee, and she's leaning against his shoulder. Tear tracks stand out on her cheeks.

Tear tracks.

"Get out," I hiss.

Kendall smiles at me smoothly as Nurrin's eyes fly open. Relief and fury war for dominance, but I dismiss her and focus on Kendall.

"Where have you been, O'Malley?" he asks, standing. "I thought we'd get you settled into your house today."

"Get the fuck out of my hotel room, Kenny. I'm too tired for your bullshit."

"I'm here because she invited me."

I cock my head, ignoring the anger at the truth in his statement. Anger later. Get rid of him *now*.

"You know what I find so odd? That you're turned on by a girl who looks like your dead sister. Even in our world, Ken, that's some twisted shit."

Rage blooms in his eyes, and Nurrin makes a choked little sound.

"Nurrin, darling, I'll see you later," he says softly, not looking away from me.

She doesn't protest when he leaves. Just watches me with big eyes as he moves closer to the door. I block it with my body and lean into him. "I am very, very good at killing. And killing you would make me very, very happy. Stay the fuck away from her, or I will see you fed to the Horde before I leave this godforsaken haven. Do you understand me?"

"I'm Kelsey's brother," he snaps. "And the fucking president."

"That means a hell of a lot less now than it did when Andrew wore the title. And Kelsey couldn't stand you, so don't think that will stay my hand. Or have you managed to block that little tidbit as well?"

"You bastard," he snarls.

I smirk. I've spent years embracing the fact that I'm a bastard. It's more of a compliment than anything else now. In our world, bastards survive. And I am nothing if not a survivor.

"Kendall, go. I need to talk to O'Malley," she says, her voice clear and startling both of us. His face goes red—being dismissed by a girl with no name or title has *got* to piss him the fuck off.

It makes me ridiculously happy.

Until the door closes, and I'm left alone with her. She's still wearing the dress from earlier, a red dress with a short skirt and thin straps that leave her shoulders bare. I was right. The scratches have formed thin scars. Her first scars.

"What the hell are you doing?" she asks, her voice shaking with fury.

"Oh, Nurrin. You don't get to ask me that. Where have you been today? Touring the Haven on the arm of America's favorite bachelor? Do you have any idea how disgusting it is, that he sees his dead sister in you and wants you?"

"Because you are so much better? You've used me as a stand in for Kelsey since we left the Hole. You only want me because you can pretend I'm her. If you want to talk about sick fucks, let's look a little closer to home."

"You have no idea what you're talking about," I say, my voice even. "So maybe you should stop. Focus on the things you know."

"I know you want me," she taunts.

I force a laugh. "I don't want Kendall's leftovers, Nurrin. Don't delude yourself."

She gasps, and I start to turn away from her. I can't be with her. The fighting wasn't enough—I want to push until she's screaming, until we're both at each other's throats, until she shatters against me. I can't—it can't happen. We can't happen. I step away, and she lunges. I twist as we fall, catch her against my chest. She's furious, spitting mad as she swings at me.

"Coming at my back? Dirty fighting, little girl," I taunt.

"What the hell is wrong with you? Why do you have to be such an asshole about *everything*? If you don't want me, why the hell does it matter if Kendall does? He could—"

"What," I hiss, my hands on her hips now. I want to shake her. "He could take care of you? Protect you? He's a weakling, Nurrin. He couldn't protect himself, much less you. You have no idea what he's capable of—he's weak, and he's got just enough power to be dangerous. Stay the fuck away from him."

"You don't get to give me orders, O'Malley," she snaps furiously.

She shifts on me, and even though we're fighting—maybe because we're fighting—I groan as her heat hits my erection. Because the second her weight landed on me, the second I felt every inch of her pressed against me, even furious and ready to gauge my eyes out, I wanted her.

I always want her. I always want this.

Her eyes drift shut as she rubs against me, almost like she doesn't realize what she's doing, and her fingers, braced on my shoulders, dig in. No gentleness. Not here. Not between us. Never between us. I thrust against her, and she groans, a throaty noise that hits me just right.

I need to erase him. I need his touch on her, his memory next to her, gone. I need her here, fully in this moment.

I rip the dress. She jerks, stunned, her eyes narrowed on me as I yank her bra down and rear up.

Then her cry is in my ears, her hands in my hair, her tit in my mouth. She's rocking against me, and I want her panties gone, I want these fucking pants gone. I want to slide deep into her. I bite down on her, and she screams, a throaty, broken noise that I want to hear every night for the rest of my life.

A dangerous thought.

I roll her off me and smack her butt lightly. "Hold on to the table," I order. She blinks, and I see the questions starting to surface in her eyes. Not what I want. I want her too lost in *this* to question me.

I dip my head down, lick at her nipple until it pebbles, and then I draw on it, sucking hard enough that she's writhing and whimpering. I bite, and she arches off the floor.

"Hold. On," I repeat. And she does.

I don't let myself think about this, because then I'd have to stop.

And I want this too damn bad.

I tug the dress until it slips from her then nudge her until she's lying on her stomach.

Then I kiss her. Starting with her scar, taking note of every shiver and stifled moan as I trace the curve of her spine. All the way down to where her back flares to meet her ass.

Just exactly as I had imagined. Little nips of teeth and the stroke of my tongue on her satin smooth skin, and I will go to hell for betraying Collin's trust like this, but I don't regret it. I can't regret it.

I will go to hell a thousand times over to have this woman in my arms for even a fraction of a moment.

I tease her until she's almost sobbing, until my name is a plea and a curse and she's thrashing under me. Then I slide up, brace myself above her. She groans as I thrust against her, and I can feel her heat, even through the two layers of clothing we're wearing. I reach between us as I thrust again, and slip two fingers through her wet heat.

And she screams, coming apart as I shove my fingers into her, the contractions of her pussy drawing me deeper. I flick my thumb over her clit, and she makes a noise, something between a moan and a whimper, bucking weakly against me as her body shudders.

For a long time, we lie like that, not speaking, my fingers still buried in her. She squeezes lightly, and I rub against her silken walls until she purrs like a kitten. I'm tempted—so fucking tempted—to coax her back to that peak, to tease her into begging.

Instead, I slip free of her and push myself off the ground. Adjust my dick in my pants as Nurrin tugs her bra up and shoves her hair out of her eyes. She's staring at me with a mixture of fascination and revulsion.

Always a good look to see in the eyes of the girl you just got off.

"Tomorrow, I'm reaching out to Omar. The Order is hiding something."

"Kendall wants you to meet with the Science Czars," she says quietly.

I go still, and then, very quietly, "Why?"

She pushes up off the floor. Even in the shreds of her dress, with her hair a mess and a sheen of sweat on her, she looks glorious. A tiny frown is on her face. “I might have mentioned that the Horde seemed to be changing.” She bites her lip. “I didn’t think it would be a problem. You’ve told everyone you could get to listen.”

I have. And it shouldn’t be. But this is 1. And they have always ignored my warnings. I told them. Kelsey and I both told them Columbus was dangerous. Omar, though—he had advocated for it, and he was our senior, in age if nothing else. And Buchman listened to him.

I shrug. “Fine. I’ll meet with him. But we’re not here to deliver warnings, Nurrin. We’re not here to court politicians. Especially not this politician.”

“Why do you hate him so much?” she asks suddenly. I shrug a little. Because he was too much of a memory, too much Kelsey, while being not nearly enough. Because Kendall spent his entire childhood hating me and blaming me for something that I hated and blamed myself for. Hating him was easier than looking in the mirror.

I don't say any of that. I lick my lips, taste her, and see her eyes go sleepy.

"He's dangerous, Nurrin. And he's not our problem. Collin is why we're here. The only reason. Don't forget that."

Her eyes go wide, and I have a moment to consider I might have gone too far, but I shove it aside and stretch, popping my sore back. "I'm taking a shower. Tomorrow will be an early morning."

I don't look back as I leave the room.

Looking back only ever gets you regrets and death.

Part 4. The Science of Change

Change is the law of life.

John F Kennedy .

We change. We adapt. The biggest change we allowed was letting fear dictate our lives—and zombies didn't do that. We did.

-Finn O'Malley .

Chapter 40. The Nature of Change

We all live in stasis. In a kind of floating state that gives us the impression that because things haven't changed, they never will. When the zombies rose, that delusion was shattered, for a time. But humanity is made up of creatures, and all of us are creatures of habit.

Falling into stasis was inevitable, as easy as breathing. Each Haven was its own self-contained world. Of course some things changed from one Haven to the next and supplies would be brought in from Havens that specialized in other things. But for the most part, we lived apart, and we were all able to convince ourselves that the world was only as big as the horizon at the edge of the Wide Open.

But that's not true. And we know it, when we allow ourselves to think about it.

Every once in a while, there is something that happens, something that is so catastrophic that we are forced to examine who we are, and why we are. What makes us different from the people around us, and what separates us from the infects.

It's a painful place to be. Change is never easy, but self-examination? That fucking hurts.

Chapter 41. The Morning After

The air feels different now. After the incident in the barracks, even then I was able to ignore the simmering attraction. He was furious. I was horny. Nothing but biological needs being met, just like Finn said.

I can't say that now. Not when there is someone who wants me, who I sent away. To fall in fucking Finn O'Malley's arms. What the hell is that? What weird life am I living?

And there was his comment, afterward—the one about Collin. How had I managed, even for an instant, to forget my brother? Was I so fucking shallow that I had been distracted by a pretty face and a charming boy? I roll to my side. 1 is dangerous. It's seductive and beautiful—lies wrapped in their glittering lights and open air restaurants. And that makes it dangerous.

Someone bangs on the door to the suite, and I tense. I'm tempted to let Finn decide to answer it, but I know, deep in my gut, who it is and what it's about. I sigh and slip out of bed. Grab my robe from the end of the bed—the Embassy provides robes. What the hell *is* that? Wrapped in the white fluffy material, I shuffle to the front of the suite.

Kendall's Walkers all have a stylized S on their shoulders. I picked up on that quickly, the small signal that symbolizes their loyalty to Stiles. I don't know if they share their loyalty with the Walkers, but first and foremost, they belong to Kendall.

"He wants you," the Walker announces. "Now, please."

I force a smile, even though I'm bristling inside. That he thinks he can snap and I will immediately jump to his demands is more than a little bit annoying.

"Why?"

The Walker blinks, startled. "Does he want to talk about the Horde or O'Malley's thoughts on them? Or perhaps the missing Black Priest who has my brother?"

"I…I don't know, ma'am."

"Tell President Stiles I'll be in his office at noon. With O'Malley. To discuss the Horde with his czars."

Confusion fills the Walker's eyes, and a kind of dislike that makes me shiver. I'm defying his boss—and he doesn't like that at all.

I step back into my room, letting the door fall gently shut.

I wait, counting silently. I'm reaching twenty and getting nervous when I finally hear him start walking away. I let out my breath and let my shoulders slump.

"Why didn't you go?"

The air crackles with tension between me and him, and I take a deep breath before turning. O'Malley is propped against the door jam, a pair of sleep pants hanging low on his waist. There's a trace of stubble on his jaw, and it hits me that his hair is getting long.

He watches me watching him, and a tiny smile tilts his lips. Shit. I've been staring too long.

"Why didn't you go?" he repeats, softly this time. Letting the question wash over me like a balm.

"Because I want to find Collin, and I can't do that while I hang on Kendall's arm." I shrug and tuck my robe tighter around me. Not that it matters. Finn has seen me nearly naked, writhing for his touch.

Heat crawls up my neck. I doubt I'll ever forget the intense, brand-like pleasure that came from giving myself over to his touch.

I do know I'll never forget the intense humiliation that swept me afterward, when I couldn't drag myself away from him. When his fingers were still buried in me, rubbing—

He growls, and I flush, looking away. "So. Noon. The czars. You can fit that into your schedule, I assume?" My voice is just a little bit too hyper. He nods, slowly, and I force a smile. "Great."

I bolt past him, and I hear him sigh my name, but I can't—I can't look at him, not when I can still feel the ghost of his touch, not when I want it again, so bad I can taste it. Not when I know he only wants to keep me from Kendall.

I fumble into the shower and turn the spray all the way to hot. Toss my robe and the bra and panties I slept in to the side and step into the water. It cascades over me, a wet embrace, and I lean my head back, letting the water soak my hair and pull it long and straight. Then I sag to the side, my head against the cool tiles, and try so hard to forget.

I want to forget Kendall, and 1, with all its wonders that will make any Haven pale in comparison. I want to forget the Order, milling around the party two nights ago, with their curious eyes and too sweet smiles. I want to forget the meeting with the czars and the behavior of the Horde, the way they've gone from small groups to a mass we have no hope of fighting.

Mostly, I want to forget the feel of Finn O'Malley whispering kisses over my skin, his body hot and heavy as it held me down, the barely restrained violence in his touch, the too strong grip of his hand on my hip. I groan, reaching between my legs, and the second I slip two fingers inside my pussy, my thumb rubbing my clit, I shatter. My legs give out, and I slide down the side of the tub and lie there, panting softly as the water swirls around me.

So much for forgetting.

Chapter 42. Panel of Czars

When I emerge from the bedroom, Finn is waiting, and from the tightness of his jaw, he’s not happy about it.

He never is. "Sorry," I say, blushing.

His eyebrows shoot up, and he laughs. "Don't do that."

"What?"

"Act like shit’s changed. Nothing's changed, Nurrin."

"How can you say that? You were there, last night— "

"Nothing. Do you understand?" he demands fiercely, standing. He's tense, a step away from lashing out, and I take a deep breath, letting it out slowly. No. I don't understand. I never do, though.

"Fine," I say, shrugging. "Nothing happened."

He stares at me for a moment longer, as if assessing me, and I lift my chin, glaring at him.

He nods and smirks. Some of the tension eases out of him. "Let's go, then."

We stop for coffee on the way out of the Embassy, and I inhale the warm steam as I follow him out of the hotel. I'm more than aware of the dirty looks we're getting, and I glance sideways at Finn. "Where were you, yesterday? Did you get in a fight with an infect?"

"Nurrin. You know that one infect hardly makes a fight."

I snort, and a smile flashes for a second. Finn looks away, and startles me when he answers. "Went to the clubs. I needed to work out some anger, and it seemed a better idea than beating Kendall to a pulp."

"Why do you hate him?" I ask, again. Finn gives me that blank stare I know so well, and I sigh, sipping my coffee. "He really isn't so bad, O'Malley. A bit arrogant, but I'm used to sharing the front seat with an ego the size a person."

"He works too closely with the Order. He's the first president in our history to appoint the Order to his cabinet. Do you realize that half the czars we're talking to are Priests? I know you want me to tolerate him, and I'll try. Mostly to make you shut the fuck up. But he's dangerous and would happily see you dead. That means he will never have a big fan in me."

"Does that still matter?" The question slips out before I can assess the wisdom of asking it, or the reasons.

Finn's gaze darts to mine. "It is the only thing that matters."

My heart twists, the idiotic thing.

“Any word on the house?” I ask. Awkward change of subject, check. Finn’s shoulder’s shake, amused, and then he shrugs.

“I’m going there after the meeting. The Embassy probably won’t tolerate me staying there for much longer.”

I should ask why, but I don’t.

"Am I going with you?" I ask softly.

He pauses on the walkway, the coffee halfway to his lips. Cocks his head to one side as he stares at me.

"You tell me, Nurrin. Are you?"

I get the feeling that we aren't talking about leaving the Embassy, and it pisses me off, a little, that he would doubt for a second that I'm committed to finding Collin. And anger is easy—it's a natural state, when dealing with Finn.

"You aren't the only one who cares about Collin, O'Malley. You don't have a patent on that—he's my brother, remember?"

His eyebrow goes up, that classic expression of disdain.

"Don't forget, Nurrin."

The office that serves as Kendall's seat of power is a plain building. A few Walkers patrol outside, and there is a receptionist at the front who gives me a frosty look as I stride up with

Finn. We're both dressed down, something that maybe wasn't the best choice considering we're meeting with the leader of the United States.

But dresses seem inappropriate after last night, and my leathers make me comfortable—less vulnerable. I need all of that I can get.

"We have a meeting with President Stiles," I say, and she wrinkles her nose.

"You can have a seat in the waiting room. He'll be back soon."

My mouth falls open, and I start to sputter something, but Finn catches my elbow, drawing me away from her and into the small waiting room. I shake him off and glare at the tiny, neatly appointed room. "Who the hell has a fucking waiting room?" I demand, pacing the little room.

"Sit down. He wants to get a rise out of us—and you are playing directly into his hands."

I dart a glance at him and meet the cool gaze.

How did I think, ever, that he was unemotional and detached? There is so much brewing in that familiar stare. He nods at the seat next to him, and I take his lead. Sit quietly, hiding behind a façade of composure.

“Good girl,” he murmurs, and I almost preen under his soft approval.

“Why is he making us wait?”

“Because he can,” Finn says quietly. He leans back in his chair, his arm brushing mine. I should move away, but I don’t. I stay exactly the way I am. “Kenny is obsessed with having what others don’t. He always has been.”

That isn’t fair.

"It's been a long time, O'Malley," I say. "You've changed since you left 1. Isn't it possible that he has too?"

He looks at me, his eyebrows raised slightly. "No. He hasn't. If he had, chasing you would not have been his first choice of action. He would have respected that you are with me."

I blink. "I'm not. We aren't together, Finn. We're together for now because circumstances dictate it. But we're not—" I break off. I don't know what to say, don't know how to say this. How to put up the barriers between us that have always been there.

"I hated you," I whisper. "It was easier, to hate you."

He touches my hand with two fingers, gently. "I know, Nurrin. Keep hating me. If that's what you need, keep hating me."

His touch is hot, like a brand, and I want to catch it in my own, wrap my fingers in his.

Is hating him easier? Because this, the idea of being with him—it seems very easy, and impossible, all at the same time. And how is that even possible? I shiver and look away.

"What happens next?"

"We take whatever information he can give us, and we go find Collin."

I roll my head to look at him. "That's not what I meant, and you know it."

He sighs and rubs a hand through his hair. It's long enough now that some of it spikes up in the front. "Let's worry about Collin. What comes after that will depend on how long we take to find him."

It's the first time he's even hinted that we might not. I think we both have been avoiding that, but it's inevitable that we'll have to deal with it.

The longer it takes, the slimmer the chances of finding Collin alive becomes.

"What do you think happened to Dustin?" I ask, my mouth dry.

Finn shrugs. "He was infected before we left Hellspawn. We all knew it. I think we were hoping for the best, but it's hard to hope for that when infection is raging like it was. That Collin kept him alive long enough to get to 9 is a miracle. He wouldn't chance Dustin turning—he would have put him down before he could."

I want to argue.

"Why can't you ever say something that doesn't make sense," I grumble, slouching in my seat.

He laughs a little, and my lips twitch. Footsteps sound down the hall, and we both straighten.

It hits me that whatever else is between us, we're in *this* together. We're partners. And maybe it's not the partnership I would have chosen, but it's the one that keeps me safe, and he's the one who won't give up on my brother.

"President Stiles will see you now," the receptionist says, her expression borderline hostile. I flash her a smile as I stand, and stalk out of the room. Finn is watching my ass—I can feel his gaze on me—but I don't particularly care in this moment.

Kendall is in a large room, sitting at the head of a table. There are four Gray-robed Priests, one Priestess, and two men in suits sitting with him. The familiar fear of the Order simmers in my veins, but I keep moving.

Half the battle is pretending until it's real.

Kendall is wearing a suit, his hair combed back, a file open in front of him. Right now, he looks like a president. It's a little disarming how much.

"Oh good. So glad you were both able to make it this morning. Sit down." He barely looks at me as we enter, as Finn nudges me forward, toward a seat. I move by instinct rather than actual intent.

He puts himself between me and the priests. Even if these aren't particularly interested in finding new Firsts to sacrifice, they are the Order. Finn doesn't trust the Order any more than I do.

Kendall makes a final note then fixes his brown eyes on us. "What do you know about the Horde's behavior pattern?"

I lean back, letting Finn have the floor. He understands the science of it better than I do, which probably stems from being the son of the world's premier scientist.

But the science isn't making an impression on Kendall. His gaze is uninterested and wandering—he doesn't care what Finn has to say.

"You aren't listening," I interrupt, "which means this is a waste of time. And I'm sorry—maybe you're okay with wasting people's time, because you're the president and you think that's okay. But I'm looking for someone, and every second you waste ignoring the warnings we don't have time to give is another second I've wasted not looking for him, and is another second closer to losing him." I cock my head.

"You lost a sibling to the infects. You should understand my worry."

Kendall's gaze is cool. "We have all lost someone, Nurrin. You're being willfully ignorant if you think otherwise."

"And you're being stubborn and childish if you ignore O'Malley's warnings just because of a childhood grudge," I say softly. There is a sharp intake of breath down the table, and O'Malley whistles at my side. I didn't mean to say that. I wasn't thinking.

Kendall fixes me with a icy stare and says, almost absently, "Everyone get out. I'd like a moment with Nurrin."

Finn laughs, an ugly noise, and Kendall's eyes flash. "Go," I murmur, quietly enough that only he hears me. The others are already leaving. I think a few are actually eager to go. "Talk to the czars. Make them listen."

"Remember what I said, Nurrin. He's dangerous."

I force a smile, and Finn heaves a sigh. Then he follows the science czars from the room, and I'm alone with Kendall.

Chapter 43. Empty Warnings

Some of the coldness drops away when we're alone, and I relax a little. "What the hell are you doing, Nurrin?" he asks quietly.

"I could ask you that," I shoot back. "You're playing games, and I don't have time for that, nor the inclination. My brother will die if we waste time, and we gave some that we don't have to tell you what the Horde is doing. And you don't care. Why?"

"Because the Horde isn't my problem. Finding a cure—that has to be our goal."

"A cure isn't feasible. You heard O'Malley—the virus is too volatile and unstable. There's no way you can get ahead of it long enough to create a cure."

"Finn doesn't know what he's talking about."

I laugh. "Even you know that's not true, Kendall. If anyone is qualified to talk about ERI, it's him."

"Because his mother created the plague? Do you think that's actually something we should value him for? The entire family is cursed. From his uncle Keifer right down to Finn O'Malley."

It's dirty—and Finn will probably kill me for it—but it's finnformation, and that is too rare to pass up.

"Tell me what you mean," I demand.

"What will you give me? Why should I?"

"Because it's the right thing to do, Kendall. Not because you'll get anything."

A smile twitches the corners of his lips, and I sigh. "Dinner. Tonight."

He nods. "Keifer was arrested twenty years earlier—when Sylvia was in her freshman year of college. They'd know for years he was a violent person. According to the files, he was prone to depression and fits of rage. When Sylvia left home, he snapped. Mass shooting at a mall in Scotland. Ten injured, three killed. He was arrested right after. And Sylvia, brilliant mind that she was, immediately went to work on a drug that could suppress the violence. Except, that's not all it did. You know what happened—she created ERI, and our government got their hands on it. That was through Griffin O'Malley. He was friends with my dad. The drug was perfect for the military, wasn't it? It was great—until it wasn't."

That's usually the way it works.

It all started with him. The brother of the scientist, the uncle. It really was the story of a family, love that was just too little, too late.

No wonder he was so distant from the rest of the world—everyone who had ever been close to him had done something completely unforgiveable.

"Just because his family did horrible things, doesn't mean he's wrong," I say. "And those horrible things weren't done with this in mind."

"Do you think that matters?" Kendall demands furiously. "They unleashed a fucking apocalypse, but because that wasn't the intention, it's okay? Do you have any idea how wrong you are?"

"Do you? Sylvia created something for a brother she loved, who did something horrible. She took that violence from him. If ERI had been left there, would we be living in this world? Or would it have died, and died again, with Keifer Cragen? But it didn't because Griffin was friends with a general in the Untied States, a war hero who heard about this amazing drug, and thought about how it could benefit his own soldiers. That wasn't something Sylvia pushed on us. Taking it to Stanlos—that wasn't something Sylvia came up with."

Rage colors his cheeks, and I murmur the last bit. "Sylvia didn't order those bombs dropped on Atlanta."

Because that's the simple truth of it. Finn's family can be blamed for a lot. But the Buchman family played their own part in the end of the world, and not all of their choices were good ones.

"It's very easy to judge someone when you aren't in their shoes, and you don't have to make the choices they do."

I tilt my head to the side, studying him. "Yes. It is."

Kendall flushes and looks away. "What does he think is so fucking important?"

"The Horde is growing. They aren't traveling in packs of ten anymore. They're moving in herds of hundreds. And ten—a few Walker's can put down ten infects without much effort. But when a Horde four or five thousand strong hits a Haven’s walls? They can't fight that—and that's when it's a small horde. If they continue to move like that—in a horde that just grows with each death—the Havens will fall. Every single one of them will fall. Even this one."

He shakes his head. "We haven't had a breech in over three years. 1 is unassailable."

I stare at him, and I wonder if he has any idea how incredibly arrogant and naive he sounds.

"We thought that the dead rising was impossible. But they did. If you sit behind these walls, content to believe that they will always protect you, they will fall. And you will die. And even if you don't, you'll be the leader of a country of the dead—because you're doing nothing to protect your people. Seven havens have already fallen."

"It's not unusual to lose a Haven occasionally."

"It wasn't unusual, when the Havens were first being built. But now? Losing seven? That's unheard of, and you know it. Don't bury your head in the sand on this one. If you do, they'll remember your name, just like they remember Keifer and Sylvia and Emilie."

That's harsh—maybe it's too harsh—but it's out. I turn away, stalking to the door.

"I'll send my man to escort you to the white house at eight." I freeze and twist to stare at him. There's a thin smile on his lips, and he shrugs. "A minor disagreement doesn't mean I don't want to see you, Nurrin."

I almost point out that this isn't a minor disagreement. But I don't—I nod once then go to Finn. "Let's get the hell outta here," I mutter to him. I feel his surprise, the way he starts to turn, to look at Kendall. "No. Just. Let's go."

"What happened?" he asks softly. A Priest is eyeing us, and Finn gives the man a tight smile, steering me toward the exit.

"Always with the fucking questions, O'Malley," I parrot back at him, mocking.

It startles a laugh out of him, and I smirk. It helps, hearing him laugh.

Chapter 44. The House on the Edge of the Wall

Finn's house is something of a shock. Because it's not a house. It's a turret, on the southeastern corner of the Wall. I stare at it, squinting against the sun still bright in the sky. "I don't get it," I say finally.

"What is there to get?" he asks, annoyed.

"Why on earth would you want to live on the Wall?"

He sighs. "This is one of the few remaining structures of the original Haven walls. Do you get that?"

"I'm not an idiot," I snap. "I can see that it's old as fuck. What I don't understand is why you got so pissy that Kendall moved your shit out."

He gives me a dirty look—which, honestly, is a step up from his blank one—and steps into the tiny house. I heave a sigh and follow him.

It's…cozy. Or cramped. Cramped is actually more accurate. The room is maybe ten by twelve, enough room to fit a bed and a table. The windows have been bricked over, with only thin slits to shoot from. There is no view of the sun, not on either side.

There is nothing that says Finn, nothing that tells me why this place matters to him more than any other. He walks the length of the room—a few steps—and then twists, peering out the slit window.

"Why is it special?" I ask. I expect him to ignore me. Because that's what O'Malley does. I ask questions; he ignores them. It's not exactly a working relationship, but it's ours, and we make it work. Most of the time.

"We grew up here," he says, startling me. "I spent the first seven years of my life exploring Scotland. The whole world was mine. Kelsey had nine years of it. And then everything changed, and this haven became our entire world. Back then, it wasn't what it is now. It was a hovel. We were attacked all the fucking time. This was our place—it wasn't attacked a lot. So we spent our time here, and the Walkers kind of adopted us. We grew up in the middle of a war our parents started, and we were forgotten the best of times."

I move, and he jerks, blinking at me. There are so many questions I want to ask, but I don't want to do anything that will make him quit talking. So I stay silent. He stares for a long minute before he shrugs.

"When she died, she gave me this place. Andrew formally gave it to her when she took her post in the army. And when I came back, he offered it to me. But I left, and I guess Kendall doesn't much care about what his family wanted, now that they're dead."

"He has a lot of anger, doesn't he?"

Finn snorts a laugh. "He's survived this long. It's kind of inevitable that he does. I have my own share of anger."

"But you channel it well." I step up to the window slit, peering out. There are a few infects darting along the road. One snaps at her pack mate then screams, jerking around and throwing herself at the Wall.

"I fight, Nurrin. And I kill."

I shrug. I don't want to argue with him about why that works. "When are you talking to Omar?"

"This evening. Kendall didn't have any information?"

"No. But maybe he will tonight."

Finn goes very still, and I freeze. Shit. I didn't mean to let that slip out, not like that.

"Why would he have anything for you tonight, Ren?" he asks, his voice silky.

"Don't get pissy," I huff. "It was an exchange. Information, and I'll have dinner with him."

He doesn't move, but I can feel him pulling away from me, his icy walls going up. I sigh. "Just what the hell kind of information do you think is so valuable that you'll spend time with him," Finn demands. "Did you forget the conversation we had about him being dangerous?"

"I didn't forget anything, O'Malley,"I snap, furious suddenly. "I did what I had to."

"What. Information?"

Oh, he will *hate* this.

I bite my lip, and Finn growls, jerking me around to face him.

"You," I yell. "It was information about you. Because I can't get it from you—and I'm tired of being the only fucking person in this god-forsaken country who doesn't know who the hell you are."

"Goddammit, Nurrin!"

"What?" I scream, shaking him off and slapping his chest. "What the hell does it matter? Why do you hide who you are?"

"Because it's *not who I am,"* he yells back. I go quiet, shrinking away from his sudden outburst. Stare at him as he struggles to rein in his temper. "That's where I came from, and shit that happened that I can't control. It's not me, Nurrin. It never was. I thought you knew that by now."

There's something in his eyes that bothers me—disgust. Disappointment. "Finn," I say, but he shakes his head.

"Don't." He walks over to the door. "I asked for one thing from you. Trust. And you couldn't fucking do that—you couldn't just wait for me, you had to know, on your terms, in your time."

"Trust goes two ways, Finn," I say, my voice shaking.

He stares at me. "I trusted you with my life, Nurrin. I trusted you to protect me when we were in the Wide Open, and to keep your mouth shut in the Stronghold, and to not shoot me when you thought I had a live virus in 18. I trusted you in that Clean house, to keep quiet and not give us away. Don't tell me I haven't trusted you."

I'm quiet, speechless. Because I can't—*no*. That wasn't trust. That was necessity. That was circumstance. He shakes his head. "I'll see you after you meet with Kenny. I hope it was worth the information you bought."

And even though logic tells me he's just going searching for information, it feels much more final when he walks away this time.

Chapter 45. Offerings

I've cleaned the room—I can't bring myself to call it a house—top to bottom and swept the floor five times. I'm going stir crazy, and it's only been a few hours since Finn abandoned me. There's a tap on the door, and I jerk, almost lunging off the bed to yank it open.

A street urchin is standing there. He's chewing on a slice of apple, a damp rag in his hand implying there are more. My stomach rumbles, reminding me loudly that I haven't eaten today. The boy eyes me curiously, and then, "Ms. Claire wants to see the O'Malley."

"Finn isn't here," I say automatically.

He shrugs, unconcerned. "Come on then."

I hesitate, and he gives me a fierce scowl. "I don't get my chocolate if I don't bring someone back. So get moving."

I glance back halfheartedly, but there's no reason to stay. Not really. Finn isn't here, and

I'm learning nothing. So I grab my gun and knives then follow the boy as I tuck the weapons into my holster.

He gives me a few curious looks as we walk, and the second time my stomach rumbles, a faintly disapproving look. Grudgingly, he extends an apple slice and gives a snort of disgust when I try to turn him down. Feeling strangely guilty, I take the fruit and munch on it as he leads me into a small neighborhood.

The house we finally approach is small, a dull green, with a neatly tended plot of grass. The street boy darts up the stairs, and I follow a little slower as he banks inside, bellowing out that he brought someone back. I hear the warm, high tones of a woman, and then he comes darting past me down the hall, clutching a bar of dark chocolate, a wide smile on his face.

"Come on in," she calls. I take a few tentative steps into a small kitchen.

Small my ass. It's a kitchen, and it's almost twice the size of Finn's entire *house.*

"So, you're the lovely bit he brought home. Haven't been able to find out much about you, except you caught the President's eye."

She's a thin, older woman with bright eyes and a wealth of lines around her smiling mouth.

She looks like someone's grandmother, a shrewdly assessing one.

"He's done every fucking thing he can to protect you. So why don't you tell me why?"

A grandmother with no tact and a potty mouth.

"Who are you, exactly?"

She smiles, a toothy grin. "Claire Donal, of Glasgow. I got stuck here when the virus broke and planes were grounded. O'Malley the senior found as many of us as he could and tried to give us a home."

"Did it work?"

She shrugs. "This isn't about me, girl."

"Why did you want him?"

Her eyes brighten. "He was looking for a few things. And I found them."

My heart jerks. "*Where?*"

Her eyes widen. "What is so important about this?"

No. She isn't playing games, not now, not when my brother is so close. "Did you find him?" I demand, lurching forward a step.

Her gaze goes soft and apologetic. "No, sweet girl. I didn't. I may have some leads—and Finn will want to check them out. But there are no promises."

She pulls a notebook off her table. It's a ratty, overstuffed thing, with notes and pieces of paper sticking out of the top and sides. She handles it with practiced familiarity, without the caution I would use, and flips toward the back. Plucks a slip of paper from the pages and hands it to me. "Finn left the house full of his belongings. This is where he'll find it—Kendall didn't have it thrown out. I don't think he had the guts."

I nod, taking the paper. "But—"

She sighs. "A priest came into the Haven three nights ago. He wasn't in robes, so most don't know he's associated with the Order. He met with a few of the Reds and spent two nights in the brothel. And he had a meeting with a few government officials."

"How do you know this?" I ask, my mouth dry.

She smiles coolly. "It's my business to know things, sweet girl. Just like I know that you matter to Finn for some reason, or he would have not gone to such lengths to hide you. How many in the Haven know you are a First?"

I freeze, and Claire smiles. "That's what I thought."

"What do you need that information for?" I ask weakly.

"I don't," she says. "I wanted to satisfy my own curiosity."

I stare at her, and she smiles gently. "Sweet girl. Finn is a Scots. He's my kinsman, because we share that. If he wants you protected, no one will learn anything about you from me. And the more I know, the more I can misdirect."

"Why does Finn not trust people?" I ask. Logic and our most recent argument tells me to shut my mouth, but I've never been very good at listening to logic.

Claire frowns a little. "You are a First—you've never known a world different from this one. And I'm—well, I was grown. I didn't have the magic of childhood wrapped around me, buffering me from the world. Finn did. And then, in one day, his mother was dead and the world was falling apart, and nothing was ever the same. He wasn't born to the world, but he was shoved into it as a child. Back then, a lot of promises were made—good intentioned things, but shit that could never be kept. Finn heard a lot of those and watched those promises be broken. He stopped trusting because the world doesn't give him much reason to."

"Does he ever lie?"

"O'Malley? On rare occasions. If it will help him keep his word. But if he's ever given you a promise, he will walk through hell to keep it."

I look away, thinking.

"What was it?" she asks quietly.

What is the only thing that matters? "He'll keep me alive. And find my brother."

She makes a soft noise, slightly surprised, and I give her a sick smile. It's all I've got at the moment. "I have to go," I say.

She watches me for a moment, and then, "Go see the Commander of the Wall. He might not be able to tell you much, but tell him I sent you and what I said. He owes me a few favors."

I nod. "Thank you."

Claire waves me away then walks me to the door. "Go on then. And try to stay alive. O'Malley has lost more than most in this world, and I'd hate to see him lose you."

There's a final question, burning on my tongue. "What happened, to Kelsey?"

Surprise flares across her face, and then her lips clamp shut and she shakes her head. "Sorry, sweet girl. There are some things even I won't trade in. When Finn is ready, he'll tell you his secrets."

No, he won't. Not after what I did today.

Chapter 46. The Commander of the Wall

Commander Orwell likes his lunch in a neat little tray, a sandwich on wheat bread, with an apple and a paring knife, and a small block of cheese.

I stare at it and think about that. A commander—the authority on military matters in the capitol—with such a simple lunch. It's not far from what we would eat in the orchards, back in Hellspawn. He catches me staring and gives me a small smile. "I've spent too many years in the field to be comfortable with the excess here. I don't judge our citizens for enjoying it—they should. We've fought hard to carve a life out of the apocalypse. But I don't forget the way my soldiers lived—the way I did."

"How did you become so powerful, here, of all places?"

He flushes. "I'm good at my job. I might not play the same game as everyone else, but I am good at keeping the Haven safe and the Walkers in top shape. When there are zombies at our door, that counts for a lot more than game playing. It's probably the only time skill is more important than game playing."

He cuts his sandwich in half and pushes half of it toward me. "I hate eating alone," he says.

I pick it up.

"Why don't you tell me why you're here," Orwell says, a not so gentle nudge.

"You know why we're here. We're looking for my brother."

"And I told O'Malley that if I came on any information, I would pass it along," he says mildly.

"Claire Donal sent me. She said you were looking for the wrong thing." His eyebrows go up, and he sits back, using the paring knife to skin the apple. I can smell the sweet fruit, and it reminds me of home. I shake the nostalgia and explain what Claire told me. A frown forms between Orwell's eyes.

"The only individual we had come to the Haven was a week ago," he says. "He was alone—you're looking for a pair."

"I don't know what he did with my brother, but the Priest was here." I fidget then ask a question that's been bothering me. "Why would the Order send in a Priest undercover?"

"They wouldn't—not for any of the other sects. But the Black doesn't have a foothold here. They won't, as long as I'm Commander. I won't let them."

"Why?"

"The Order is unpredictable and dangerous. They don't have the interest of the nation at heart. They have their own. I don't want that here. I can't do anything about the other sects—but as long as I control our military, I'll keep them at bay."

"So what would be so important that the order would smuggle one of their priests in?"

"The change in the Horde?" he suggests. I blink, and he smiles, amused. "You are not the only one to watch the patterns. We're aware of the changes."

"Then why aren't you doing anything?"

"Like what?" he says. "We can't evacuate all of the Havens. We've done that before—there is nowhere else to go."

"But if you stay," I say, "the haven will fall."

He stares at me, and I see the knowledge and acceptance in his eyes.

"Accepting it is accepting a death sentence," I whisper. "It will mean extinction, for all of us."

"Not everyone. There are a few—people like O'Malley." He cocks his head. "And you. Survivors. We'll go on, as long as we have people like you. O'Malley won't die because of an infect. He's too much of a survivor."

"A handful of people can't sustain humanity," I say.

He laughs, a little bit bitter. "We've been an endangered species since Emilie died, Nurrin. We've just been ignoring our own mortality. Build a wall high enough, build it thick enough, and people will begin to believe it's impregnable. But believing it doesn't make it true."

"Does Kendall know this?"

"Of course. He's the president."

"Then why doesn't he do something to stop it?"

"Because knowing and believing are two very different things."

Chapter 47. A Room of Regret

The turret is full of boxes. Apparently, Claire was handing out chocolate again, because there's a note from her.

Thought a delivery would be easiest. Stay alive.

C~

I'm vaguely tempted to delve into the boxes, but decide against it. I've pushed Finn's patience far enough—and I still have that stupid dinner with Kendall tonight. Maybe I can leave early.

There is a tap on the door, and I peek out. A Walker, wearing Kendall's symbol. Carrying a thin box.

"The president sent this for you, ma'am."

I take the box and give him a blank look. The Walker steps to one side of the door, assuming a loose military stance.

"What are you doing?" I ask.

"I'm to take you to President Stiles, when you're ready."

I open my mouth to argue with him, but I close it again before I can say anything. He's following orders—nothing more or less than that. Instead, I close the door quietly and move to sit on the bed. Boxes dig into my knees. I want to sleep—for just a while, I want to forget everything, the fight with Finn, and Orwell's words, the zombies—everything. Sometimes, I just want Collin, and our dirty apartment in Hellspawn, and the knowledge that as long as he was there, I wasn't alone.

I twist on the bed, staring out the window slit. The pack from earlier is dead now. A lone figure is standing out there, and I know he's human—he is too still to be anything else. I release my breath and stand.

Finn and Kendall have something in common. Both of them enjoy dressing me in ridiculous outfits.

The dress is pretty—a form fitting black sheath with a low v-neck and geometric designs cut out of the back, wrapping around my sides. The skirt is tight and short, with a sheer red overlay that is short in the front and hangs almost to my feet in the back. And heels. The man sent me fucking heels. Black boots with corset lacing up the back, that wrap to just past my knees, with a spiking heel that gives me an extra four inches of height. I touch up my makeup and leave my hair down. And run into a problem. There is nowhere for my gun. My knives are tucked into my boots, and a garrote wire is wrapped around my wrist like a bracelet. But the dress has no room for hiding.

Biting my lip, I put the gun on the bed and open the door. The Walker's eyes go wide when he sees me, and he swallows. "I'm ready to go," I say softly.

I feel like I'm on display, following the solider. In a way, I am. The other Walkers see, and I can hear the murmurs. They know where I'm going. Soon the entire Haven will.

I see Finn when we reach the base of the Wall, just before veering off toward the government district. His eyes trace over me, going dark, but when he meets my gaze, he's blank. Perfectly blank and quietly furious.

How could you?

I want to say I'm sorry. That I fucked up. I do trust him.

But I don't. I look away and follow my escort to another man. I leave Finn behind.

Chapter 48. Presidential Dinners

Kendall is in his office, which is where I am delivered. The Walker is dismissed without a second glance, and I'm alone with him. Kendall smiles at me. "That dress looks amazing on you."

"Thank you. I don't dress up often—there wasn't a lot of need for it in Hellspawn."

"A beautiful girl should always wear beautiful clothes."

I cock my head at him. "Not very practical for fighting, though."

"Which is why you have people to do that for you."

I blink. It's not me. Letting someone else take care of the infects, to not fight—that is anathema. Even in Hellspawn, my workouts were heavy on defensive maneuvers.

"Enough of that. Give me just a moment and I'll be ready."

I nod and take a step away. A few pictures are hanging on his wall, and I step closer to one. He's standing with a blonde-haired girl, his arm wrapped around her waist. They stand in a room that looks vaguely familiar.

"Ready?"

I nod, pulled from my thoughts to face Kendall. His gaze flicks past me to the picture, and then back to me. He smiles and says, "Come on, then."

There is a car waiting to drive us, and I arch an eyebrow at it. Kendall catches the expression and gives me a smile. "Privilege of the job."

He helps me into my seat, and I smile at him. "How did you get the job, anyway?"

"Well, it's something of a family tradition. My father wasn't the first to be president—there was Grandfather Stiles, about ten years before him. We've always been heavily involved in politics and the military. When it was time to elect someone, there weren't many volunteers. I was asked, and I thought I could do some good. So I said yes."

"And have you? Done good?"

Kendall gives me a bashful smile. "Some think so."

It's a non-answer. My lips curve into a smile, matching his, but I feel off. The argument with Finn is too present in my mind, his warnings and insistance that Kendall is dangerous.

"Why do you hate Finn so much?" I ask.

He's good. Nearly as good as Finn. And if I were used to anyone else, I probably wouldn't catch the small tells—the tightening of his lips, the anger flaring in his eyes. There and gone so quickly.

"How did you come to be with him?" he counters.

I shrug. "Finn was around when Hellspawn fell. We wouldn't have made it out without him."

"But why did you stay with him?" Kendall presses.

I stare. "Because he survives. Because the people around him survive."

"But he killed an Alderman."

The car comes to a gentle stop. I barely realize it—the statement is too shocking, too unexpected. Why is it unexpected? Kendall is the president of the Untied States, and even in the fractured state that we are, he knows things that happen. Things that I don't necessarily expect him to know.

Kendall helps me out of the car and holds my hand lightly as we enter the brightly lit restaurant. A few Walkers are scattered around the room. I glance around.

It's a restaurant. We had one, in Hellspawn, but it was for the wealthy—not for an orphan and her Walker brother. I've never been to a restaurant, unless you count the kink club in Vegas. Which I don't.

Vegas. The sacrifice.

I stumble, missing a step, and Kendall's grip on my hand tightens, steadying me. I want to shake him off. The pieces of the puzzle have fallen into place, and my stomach is heaving. I want to bolt.

Finn said he was dangerous, and I dismissed it. Because even though I know he's right—even though I know to trust him—I thought it was jealousy.

I'm a fucking idiot.

"Are you ok?" Kendall asks softly.

I nod, too sharp and jerky. "Of course. Sorry—these heels. I'm used to flat shoes."

"Not much farther, darling," he says, smiling and wrapping an arm around my waist. He tugs me into him and guides me to a small table. Two glasses of wine are already waiting for us. Kendall waits until I'm sitting then circles to sit across from me. I sneak a glance around—a few other couples are here, but the restaurant is mostly deserted.

What the hell is he doing? What game is he playing?

"I had the chef prepare a steak. I hope you don't mind," he says, looking vaguely apologetic. I wave it away and sip my wine. "Nurrin. I know you came here for your brother. And I want you to know I'll do whatever I can to find him—to help you find him. But if we can't—what will you do? Have you considered that?"

I stare at him blankly. "Not finding Collin isn't an option."

"But you must understand that he could be dead. That there are no guarantees."

I pick at the chain around my neck, lifting the tiny vial so that it hangs between us.

"You know what this is?"

He looks uncomfortable, but he nods. Of course he nods. He knows, just as well as anyone—we are children of this world, after all.

"This was my first boyfriend. Dustin. Collin was with him. So yes. I know—I'm aware of the lack of promises and that even when people make them, they can't be kept. I know that Collin could be dead. But I won't quit looking. Finn won't quit looking. Do you understand that as long as there is hope—as long as there is no dead body—we'll keep looking?"

"So you'll leave with him. That's what you're saying," Kendall says quietly. He's staring at me, a little too hard for my comfort. I sigh and toy with my wine glass.

"Yes. Because I trust O'Malley to find Collin."

Kendall's eyebrows go up at that, and I shrug. "You don't have to understand or agree with me, Kendall. I don't really expect you to. But I know why I'm staying near him."

"He's ruthless."

"He's also effective," I say, my voice even. I shake my head. "We could argue all night about this. But Finn is a non-negotiable. I might have my own issues with the man, but he's who I've trusted to find my brother. You can accept that or you can not, but it won't change. So,"—I lift my glass, and arch an eyebrow—"why don't we enjoy what's left of the evening?"

Kendall smiles, and if it seems a bit thin, I can understand that. I'm don't expect him to like my stance. I just expect him to back off his attack.

A server approaches with our dinner, and I stare at the red meat. Juice is swirling around the plate, too fast. My head spins, and I feel my stomach lurch dangerously.

"You gave her too much," a voice says.

"Shut up," Kendall answers. I look up and see him, still staring. His gaze is clinical, and that is more disturbing than anything else.

I forgot. For just a few seconds, I forgot, and how fucking stupid is that?

"She won't do the Priestess any good if she's dead."

"I said shut *up,*" Kendall says, snarling now. I try to stand, and the room sways drunkenly. My lips are too thick, and my voice comes out garbled when I try to speak. It doesn't make sense—nothing makes sense.

Finn.

Oh god, I forgot his warning. How stupid can I possibly be, that I would forget it, even knowing?

"Sacrifice," I gasp. Surprise flares on Kendall's face, and he laughs as the world tilts away. A tunnel of black wraps around me as I fall.

"She's a smart little bitch. Go ahead. Get it done."

Something slams into my head. Pain explodes through me. I fall into the dark.

Chapter 49. The Dark

My mouth is dry when I wake up. My mouth is dry, and my head feels like it's about to fall off. It doesn't ache—it literately feels like it will separate from my body and roll across the fucking floor, and I almost wish it would.

I can't see anything.

An unfamiliar voice murmurs, "She's awake, sir."

I hear a soft shuffle, and then, "How did you know?"

I almost scream, but I manage to keep the noise from escaping. The pain is too fierce, roaring through me, and I whimper, curling onto my bare legs. The silk of my dress is almost obscene now. "How," Kendall's voice, disembodied and too loud, repeats.

"I watched her die, you sick fuck," I gasp, and he laughs. The bastard actually fucking laughs at me.

"He actually took you to the Stronghold."

"Finn will murder you for this—slowly," I hiss.

"Finn has wanted me dead for years, Nurrin. And yet I'm alive. I'm alive and powerful while he wanders from Haven to Haven, and no one fucking cares. No one remembers that he was a hero—they only remember his mother started the apocalypse."

"Fuck you, Buchman. Your hands are just as fucking bloody."

The lights flare, and I do scream, pain lancing through me, exploding in my head. I clamp my eyes shut, willing the pain away, tears squeezing down my cheeks, until spots form behind my closed eyelids and everything fades away.

The lights are on when I come to. Kendall is sitting in the corner of the room, on the only piece of furniture—a hard-backed chair. There's a small file in his hands. I lick my lips. I'm thirsty. So thirsty. I wonder how long I've been out this time.

"What did you give me?"

"Cocktail we give all sacrifices," he says, not bothering to look up. "I've known about you for a while, Nurrin. When Priest Matthew came here with Collin, I knew it was only a matter of time before you would come here with Finn. We were prepared. I'll admit, though—I didn't expect you to be so reminiscent of Kelsey. That startled me."

"It's kind of sick, you know," I say, conversational. Kendall finally looks up, an eyebrow raised. "That your sister's look-alike is such a turn on."

Amusement flickers in his eyes, but he doesn't argue with my assessment.

"What happens now?" I demand.

"Now? We wait for the Reds. They won't be long," he says, a smile playing on his lips.

"Why do you do this?" Nothing is making sense, he's spinning, and I frown, trying to make the world settle. Why is everything spinning? "Why are you working with the Order? What's in it for you?"

Kendall smiles. "I'm president, Nurrin. Who do you suppose made that happen? You don't really believe a bunch of war heroes decided a boy who has never Walked would make a good president."

I throw up, suddenly, and he sighs. "I hate this part." He stands, and I listen to his footsteps recede as the world twists around me.

Chapter 50. Waiting

Not long is a relative term. Kendall doses me with the cocktail of drugs four times, and each time, I do the same cycle—blinding pain, burning thirst, and a disorientation. Long stretches of time are lost. I wake screaming, my throat raw and sore.

In my rare moments of lucidity, I focus on Finn. He knows—by now, he must know. He'll find me.

What is the only thing that matters?

When I drift on pain and scream through the delusions of disorientation, I can't remember why I think he'll come. The guards change, and I see Kendall less frequently. Sometimes I wake sore, finding bruises I can't account for.

Why hasn't he found me? Where the fuck is he?

We fought. We fought, and he left—maybe he's decided that he's had enough.

Maybe he's left me and 1 behind, washed his hands of Collin.

I'll keep you alive. I'll keep Collin safe.

Where is he?

Finn once said hope is the great lie. It's what we used to rally. What kept humanity going when we should have laid down and accepted our fate. I wonder if that is true.

I don't have hope. I don't need it. I have knowledge. It may take time, and I might hate every moment of the wait, but Finn will come. He will find me—and when he does, he'll wash these rooms in blood.

Hope doesn't keep me alive. Faith in him does—and the burning desire to see every last one of my tormentors dead.

Chapter 51. The Order

Something is different when I wake the sixth time. The pain is gone—but I'm not thirsty, and the only thing that moves is the ground, a steady sway.

I'm being moved.

I shiver and shift in the room. Or whatever the hell it is that I'm in. Tentatively, I reach out and touch the walls. Cool metal, vibrating slightly.

"What the hell," I murmur.

"It's a train."

The voice is weak and tired, thin with exhaustion, hoarse. But it jerks me around, so fast I hear my neck pop. The room is dark, but light flickers from overhead occasionally—a thin gap in the roof. I catch the occasional glimpse of him, and my breath catches in my throat. A sob works its way up, and Collin gives me a wry smile. "Come here, idiot."

I make a noise, and his face spasms, and then I'm across the small space, buried in his arms. And I'm crying—all the tears I haven't shed, all the ones I didn't cry over him when I first realized he was missing, or when I found Dustin dead.

"Hush, shhh." Collin shifts me so I'm resting against one arm, petting my hair awkwardly as he lets me cry myself out. And I do. For so long that I lose track of time. My eyes feel puffy, and my nose hurts, but I finally look back at him and give him a watery smile. "Where are we going? Where's Finn?"

Hope flares across his face. "You were with Finn? What happened?"

I blink. "Wait—Collin, where are we?"

"Where is O'Malley?" he demands.

"1," I say, my lips numb. I feel empty, hallowed out from crying and the sudden crash of knowledge.

I knew Finn would come for me. I knew he would find Collin. So to have one, without the other—it's unfathomable. But it's my reality. "Where are we?"

"The Order has us, Ren. I don't know where they're taking us."

Which means…I shift, away from Collin.

"He lied," I whisper.

"About what?"

I can't answer. Everything from the past few days is crashing over me, every moment I lay, drugged and hurt, believing that he would find me.

"Why did you ever trust him?" I demand, furious suddenly.

"Because there is very little in the world that he wouldn't do to keep you—and me—safe," Collin says softly. There is something off about his voice, something in those words that I can't quite fathom.

I turn to look at him, put my hand down. He flinches, and everything freezes inside me.

"Collin?" I whisper, a little girl begging for reassurance. He shifts, and I can feel tears burning in my eyes. I don't want to see this—I shake my head, and he laughs, that hoarse noise that is so off.

"How many weapons do you have?" he asks.

Not enough. Not for this. Not a gun.

"Where? How?"

He grunts, and I look behind me. It's lying on the other side of the train car, rank and rotten.

I can't bear to look at it, so I turn away. Light flashes above us again, illuminating the truth.

His leg is mangled, a mess of bloody bite marks.

I've found him, and it's not fair, because I'm not ready for this, I'm not ready to do this. Not again.

Not ever.

"Don't hide from it, Ren," he says, and I hear Finn in his voice, disgusted with my dissembling.

I take a deep breath and stare.

Collin's been bitten. My brother is going to turn.

The End.

Acknowledgements

This is always—always—the hardest part of writing my books. So here we go:

The Indie Ignites, who always make me laugh and whom I adore, and the New Adult Author Ignite, which has been such a huge help to me. I love the discussions we have and learning from y'all.

The bloggers who have loved my zombies—especially Holly, who is still terrified of them, but got behind this little book anyway. To all of the amazing bloggers who participated in my tour and blitz—I adore you. Each and every one of you.

Hailey, who keeps me sane IRL, and babysits when I'm behind on a deadline.

My amazing team, who makes me look good: Rae, who cussed over the ending, and Mel who gave Finn such a pretty back of the head, and Chantee who makes the formatting look freaking awesome. Jessica, for being such a rockstar when it comes getting the books out there.

My husband, who tolerates my fascination with zombies and words with the patience of a saint, and my gorgeous daughters, who really want me to write about a superhero. Soon, ladies.

This book would not have been possible without the encouragement I got from readers. Every week—several times a week—readers have tweeted and emailed and facebooked me, demanding to know when the next book would be out, and to tell me what they thought of Finn and Nurrin. That has been so amazing—each and every time, I've grinned and bounced a bit. I'm so happy y'all love my little zombie book as much as I do.

New adult is a developing category, and for the most part is college romance. But there is so much room for growth in our little category, and each time I see one of y'all reading this world, it gives me hope that it is growing. And that is wonderful. Thank you for reading, lovelies.

N~

About The Author

Nazarea Andrews is an avid reader and tends to write the stories she wants to read. She loves chocolate and coffee almost as much as she loves books, but not quite as much as she loves her kids. She lives in south Georgia with her husband, daughters, and overgrown dog

You can follow her on Facebook and Twitter.